he bearer of this
scroll, namely,

_____

is a master in the
Order of the Kai

The moment you draw the dagger from your belt, a blue flame courses the length of its twisted blade and the squealing flood of Crypt Spawn soar upward towards the roof in order to avoid you. They and their creator, Darklord Kraagenskûl, recognize the power you wield and both are in awe and terror of it. Freed from the threat of his loathsome summonations, you now advance upon Kraagenskûl with the dagger before you. He screams in anger and lunges at your head, his sword ablaze with tongues of black fire. You catch the blow on the tip of the dagger and both blades spark furiously as their terrible powers collide...

JOE DEVER was born in 1956 at Woodford Bridge in Essex. After he left college, he became a professional musician, working in studios in Europe and America. While working in Los Angeles in 1977, he discovered a game called "Dungeons and Dragons" and was soon an enthusiastic player. Five years later he won the Advanced Dungeons and Dragons Championships in the U.S., where he was the only British competitor. The award-winning Lone Wolf adventures are the culmination of many years of developing the world of Magnamund. They are printed in several languages and sold throughout the world.

Joe Dever Books From Berkley Publishing

The Lone Wolf Series:
Flight from the Dark
Fire on the Water
The Caverns of Kalte
The Chasm of Doom
Shadow on the Sand
The Kingdoms of Terror
Castle Death
The Jungle of Horrors
The Cauldron of Fears
The Dungeons of Torgar
The Prisoners of Time
The Masters of Darkness
The Plague Lords of Ruel
The Captives of Kaag
The Darke Crusade

The World of Lone Wolf Series:
Grey Star the Wizard
The Forbidden City
Beyond the Nightmare Gate
War of the Wizards

The Freeway Warrior Series:
Highway Holocaust
Mountain Run
The Omega Zone
California Countdown

by Joe Dever and John Grant

The Legends of Lone Wolf Series:
Eclipse of the Kai
The Dark Door Opens
The Tides of Treachery
The Sword of the Sun
Hunting Wolf

By Joe Dever and Gary Chalk

The Magnamund Companion:
The Complete Guide to the
World of Lone Wolf and
Grey Star

BOOK 12

The Masters of Darkness

Joe Dever

Illustrated by Brian Williams

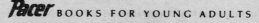

Pacer BOOKS FOR YOUNG ADULTS

BERKLEY BOOKS, NEW YORK

If you purchased this book without a cover, you should be aware that this book is stolen property. It was reported as "unsold and destroyed" to the publisher, and neither the author nor the publisher has received any payment for this "stripped book."

This Berkley/Pacer book contains the complete text of the original edition.

THE MASTERS OF DARKNESS

A Berkley/Pacer Book, published by arrangement with Century Hutchinson Ltd.

PRINTING HISTORY
Beaver Books edition published 1988
Berkley/Pacer edition / July 1989

All rights reserved.
Text copyright © 1988 by Joe Dever.
Illustrations copyright © 1988 by Brian Williams.
This book may not be reproduced in whole or in part, by mimeograph or any other means, without permission.
For information address: Arrow Books Limited, 62-65 Chandos Place, London WC2N 4NW.

ISBN: 0-425-11718-9
RL: 9.5

Pacer is a trademark belonging to The Putnam Publishing Group.

A BERKLEY BOOK ® TM 757,375
Berkley/Pacer Books are published by The Berkley Publishing Group, 200 Madison Avenue, New York, NY 10016.
The name "Berkley" and the "B" logo are trademarks belonging to Berkley Publishing Corporation.

PRINTED IN THE UNITED STATES OF AMERICA

10   9   8   7   6   5

For Sophie and Ben

With special thanks to
Adrian Orr – creator of the 'Mind Reaper'.

MAGNAKAI DISCIPLINES   NOTES

1	
2	
3	
4	4th Magnakai discipline if you have completed 1 Magnakai adventure successfully
5	5th Magnakai discipline if you have completed 2 Magnakai adventures successfully
6	6th Magnakai discipline if you have completed 3 Magnakai adventures successfully
7	7th Magnakai discipline if you have completed 4 Magnakai adventures successfully
8	8th Magnakai discipline if you have completed 5 Magnakai adventures successfully
9	9th Magnakai discipline if you have completed 6 Magnakai adventures successfully

MAGNAKAI   LORE – CIRCLE   BONUSES

	CS	EP		CS	EP
CIRCLE OF FIRE	+1	+2	CIRCLE OF SOLARIS	+1	+3
CIRCLE OF LIGHT	0	+3	CIRCLE OF THE SPIRIT	+3	+3

BACKPACK (max. 8 articles)	MEALS
1	
2	
3	—3 EP if no Meal available when instructed to eat.
4	
5	BELT POUCH Containing Gold Crowns (50 maximum)
6	
7	
8 Can be discarded when not in combat.	

CS = COMBAT SKILL   EP = ENDURANCE POINTS

ACTION CHART

COMBAT SKILL	ENDURANCE POINTS
	Can never go above initial score 0 = dead

COMBAT RECORD

ENDURANCE POINTS		ENDURANCE POINTS
LONE WOLF	COMBAT RATIO	ENEMY
LONE WOLF	COMBAT RATIO	ENEMY
LONE WOLF	COMBAT RATIO	ENEMY
LONE WOLF	COMBAT RATIO	ENEMY
LONE WOLF	COMBAT RATIO	ENEMY

MAGNAKAI RANK

SPECIAL ITEMS LIST

DESCRIPTION	KNOWN EFFECTS

WEAPONS LIST

WEAPONS (maximum 2 Weapons)
1
2

If holding Weapon and appropriate Weaponmastery in combat +3 CS. If combat entered carrying no Weapon −4CS.

WEAPONMASTERY CHECKLIST

DAGGER		SPEAR	
MACE		SHORT SWORD	
WARHAMMER		BOW	
AXE		SWORD	
QUARTERSTAFF		BROADSWORD	

QUIVER & ARROWS

Quiver	No. of arrows carried
YES/NO	

THE STORY SO FAR

You are the warrior, Lone Wolf, last of the Kai Masters of Sommerlund and sole survivor of the massacre that destroyed your kinsmen during a bitter war with your age-old enemies – the Darklords of Helgedad.

Many centuries have passed since Sun Eagle, the first of your kind, established the Order of the Kai. Aided by the magicians of Dessi, he completed a perilous quest to find seven crystals of power known as the Lorestones of Nyxator, and upon their discovery he unlocked a wisdom and strength that lay within both the Lorestones and himself. He recorded the nature of his discoveries and his experiences in a great tome entitled *The Book of the Magnakai*. You found this lost Kai treasure and gave a solemn pledge to restore the Kai to their former glory, thereby ensuring the security of your land in the years to come. To fulfil your pledge, you embarked on the same quest that was undertaken by Sun Eagle over one thousand years ago: the search for the seven crystals of power that hold the power and wisdom of your ancestors.

Your quest was to take you far from your northern

homeland. Following in the footsteps of the first Kai Grand Master you journeyed to Dessi and sought the help of the Elder Magi, the magicians who aided Sun Eagle on his quest long ago. There you learned that for centuries the Elder Magi had awaited your coming. An ancient Dessi legend told of the birth and rise to greatness of two 'Koura-tas-Kai', which means 'Sons of the Sun'. One was named 'Ikar', which means 'eagle', and the other was named 'Skarn', which means 'wolf'. A prophecy foretold that the Koura-tas-Kai would each come from out of the north to seek the counsel of the Elder Magi in order that they might fulfil a great quest. Although separated by several centuries, they would share one spirit, one purpose and one destiny — to triumph over the champions of darkness in an age of great peril. The Elder Magi knew that you were Skarn, the wolf of Dessi legend, and in keeping with their ancient vows they promised to help you complete the Magnakai quest.

In Elzian, the capital of Dessi, you were tutored in the histories of Magnamund and received lessons in lore that you would have learned from the Kai masters if only they, like you, had survived the murderous Darklord attack on the Kai monastery. You were eager to learn all that the Elder Magi could teach you in preparation for your quest, but war was to cut short your tuition. In the Darklands capital of Helgedad a struggle for power had been won by a Darklord called Gnaag. The other Darklords, fourteen in number, united behind their new leader and upon his command began to muster huge armies in preparation for the conquest of Magnamund. Swiftly their giak legions grew in number, enabling Gnaag to launch a sweeping invasion that was to catch the freelands unprepared.

His legions advanced unchecked until, at the momentous Battle of Tahou, you turned the tide of the war decisively against Gnaag by defeating his powerful ally, Zakhan Kimah, in mortal combat.

Victory at Tahou paved the way for the liberation of all the lands that Gnaag had taken by force. But the sweet taste of this victory was to turn sour when you discovered that he had captured the last three remaining Lorestones of Nyxator, and had vowed to avenge his defeat by destroying them and killing you. Alarmed by this news, the High Council of the Elder Magi helped you to formulate a plan of action. They had received news from allies in the west that the Lorestones were being held in the city-fortress of Torgar, where Gnaag's sorcerers — the nadziranim — were searching for a means of destroying them. Fearing that they might achieve their goal, the Elder Magi made preparations for your secret passage to Torgar and, after a long and perilous journey, you arrived to find it besieged by the allied armies of Talestria and Palmyrion. During the early months of the Darklord invasion, hundreds of Talestrians were enslaved and sent to labour in the dungeons and sulphur mines deep within the bowels of Torgar. Their plight had seemed hopeless until the allied armies, under the command of Lord Adamas of Garthen, finally arrived to liberate them. Due in part to your bravery and skill during the assault, Lord Adamas's troops were able to breach the great Torgar gate and storm its citadel. During this fierce battle you gained entry to the chamber at the heart of the citadel where the nadziranim were attempting to destroy the Lorestones. Above a circular black pit the three radiant gems hung suspended in a fireball of negative energy,

13

the focal point of several beams of power arising from crystals set around the edge of the pit. By means of a gantry you were able to climb above these energy beams and retrieve one of the three Lorestones. But, as you reached out for the remaining two, the terrible voice of Darklord Gnaag filled the chamber. 'Vengeance is mine!' he rasped, and in the next instant a bolt of blue lightning leapt from a crystal that he held in his fly-like hand. It sheared through the rusty iron gantry, creating a shock wave that sent the Lorestones tumbling into the black pit. A second bolt ripped the gantry in two, and, with the ghastly laugh of Darklord Gnaag ringing in your ears, you fell headlong into a portal of total darkness – a Shadow Gate – which led to the twilight world of the Daziarn Plane.

When first you looked upon the desolate wastelands of the Daziarn, you recalled what little you had heard tell of this alien world. The magicians of Sommerlund believe it to be an astral corridor, connecting and binding the planet Magnamund to other planes of existence. By passing through a Shadow Gate – one of which is situated below their Guildhall in the city of Toran – a person could gain entry to the Daziarn. However, all those who had ever passed through the Shadow Gate of Toran had never been seen again, prompting the magicians to believe that the journey could only be made in one direction. It was said that from the Daziarn there was no escape.

Your vow to restore the Kai, and your stubborn will to survive against all odds, made you even more determined to recover the last two Lorestones and find a way of returning to your home world. In the course of your search you discovered that your fight against the forces of darkness was the focus of a greater conflict raging throughout all the planes of existence, and that the time had come when the actions of one individual would shape the future of every living thing. It came as a great revelation to discover that you were that individual.

Part of your destiny was fulfilled when you fought and defeated the Chaos-master, the leader of the evil force that threatened to conquer the Daziarn. You recovered one of the Lorestones and, with the help of a god-like creature called Serocca, you were able to find the location of a Shadow Gate that would return you to your own world. Here your quest culminated in a battle with your old enemy, Vonotar the Traitor, who had found the last Lorestone and who controlled the city wherein lay the Shadow Gate. He had intended to use the power of the Lorestone to enable him to return to Magnamund, but your bravery and determination put paid to his plans. In a desperate fight, on the very threshold of the Shadow Gate itself, you slew him and retrieved the last Lorestone, thereby completing the Magnakai Quest. Instantly an overwhelming wave of power was transfused into your being, lifting you to a level of consciousness that transcended your mortal frame. You surrendered to this power and, under its guidance, you were drawn inexorably towards the Shadow Gate. Willingly you stepped into the icy darkness and began your triumphant return to the world where you were born.

THE GAME RULES

You keep a record of your adventure on the *Action Chart* that you will find in the front of this book. For further adventuring you can copy out the chart yourself or get it photocopied.

During your training as a Kai Master you have developed fighting prowess – COMBAT SKILL – and physical stamina – ENDURANCE. Before you set off on your adventure you need to measure how effective your training has been. To do this take a pencil and, with your eyes closed, point with the blunt end of it on to the *Random Number Table* on the last page of this book. If you pick 0 it counts as zero.

The first number that you pick from the *Random Number Table* in this way represents your COMBAT SKILL. Add 10 to the number you picked and write the total in the COMBAT SKILL section of your *Action Chart* (ie, if your pencil fell on the number 4 in the *Random Number Table* you would write in a COMBAT SKILL of 14). When you fight, your COMBAT SKILL will be pitted against that of your enemy. A high score in this section is therefore very desirable.

The second number that you pick from the *Random Number Table* represents your powers of ENDURANCE. Add 20 to this number and write the total in the ENDURANCE section of your *Action Chart* (ie, if your pencil fell on the number 6 on the *Random Number Table* you would have 26 ENDURANCE points).

If you are wounded in combat you will lose ENDURANCE points. If at any time your ENDURANCE points fall to zero, you are dead and the adventure is over. Lost ENDURANCE points can be regained during the course of the adventure, but your number of ENDURANCE points can never rise above the number you started with.

If you have successfully completed any of the previous adventures in the Lone Wolf series, you can carry your current scores of COMBAT SKILL and ENDURANCE points over to Book 12. You may also carry over any Weapons and Special Items you have in your possession at the end of your last adventure, and these should be entered on your new *Action Chart* (you are still limited to two Weapons and eight Backpack Items).

You may choose one bonus Magnakai Discipline to add to your *Action Chart* for every Lone Wolf Magnakai adventure you complete successfully (books 6–12).

MAGNAKAI DISCIPLINES

During your training as a Kai Lord, and in the course of the adventures that led to the discovery of *The Book of the Magnakai*, you have mastered all ten of the basic warrior skills known as the Kai Disciplines.

After studying *The Book of the Magnakai*, you have also reached the rank of Kai Master Superior, which means that you have learnt *three* of the Magnakai Disciplines listed below. It is up to you to choose which three skills these are. As all of the Magnakai Disciplines will be of use to you at some point on your adventure, pick your three with care. The correct use of a Magnakai Discipline at the right time can save your life.

The Magnakai skills are divided into groups, each of which is governed by a separate school of training. These groups are called 'Lore-circles'. By mastering all the Magnakai Disciplines in a particular Lore-circle, you can gain an increase in your COMBAT SKILL and ENDURANCE points score. (See the section 'Lore-circles of the Magnakai' for details of these bonuses.)

When you have chosen your three Magnakai Disciplines, enter them in the Magnakai Disciplines section of your *Action Chart*.

Weaponmastery
This Magnakai Discipline enables a Kai Master to become proficient in the use of all types of weapon. When you enter combat with a weapon you have mastered, you add 3 points to your COMBAT SKILL. The rank of Kai Master Superior, with which you begin the Magnakai series, means you are skilled in *three* of the weapons listed opposite and overleaf.

18

SPEAR

DAGGER

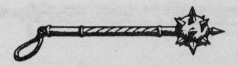

MACE

SHORT SWORD

WARHAMMER

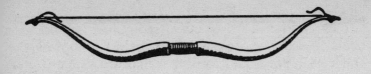

BOW

QUARTERSTAFF

BROADSWORD

AXE

SWORD

If you choose this skill, write 'Weaponmastery: +3 COMBAT SKILL points' on your *Action Chart*, and tick your chosen weapons on the weapons list that appears on page 9. You cannot carry more than two weapons.

Animal Control

This Magnakai Discipline enables a Kai Master to communicate with most animals and to determine their purpose and intentions. It also enables a Kai Master to fight from the saddle at great advantage.

If you choose this skill, write 'Animal Control' on your *Action Chart*.

Curing

The possessor of this skill can restore 1 lost ENDURANCE point to his total for every numbered section of the book through which he passes, provided he is not involved in combat. (This can only be done after his ENDURANCE has fallen below its original level.) This Magnakai Discipline also enables a Kai Master to cure disease, blindness and any combat wounds sustained by others, as well as himself. Using the knowledge mastery of this skill provides will also allow a Kai Master to identify the properties of any herbs, roots and potions that may be encountered during the adventure.

If you choose this skill, write 'Curing: + 1 ENDURANCE point for each section without combat' on your *Action Chart*.

Invisibility

This Magnakai skill allows a Kai Master to blend in with his surroundings, even in the most exposed terrain.

It will enable him to mask his body heat and scent, and to adopt the dialect and mannerisms of any town or city that he visits.

If you choose this skill, write 'Invisibility' on your *Action Chart*.

Huntmastery
This skill ensures that a Kai Master will never starve in the wild; he will always be able to hunt for food, even in areas of wasteland and desert. It also enables a Kai Master to move with great speed and dexterity and will allow him to ignore any extra loss of COMBAT SKILL points due to a surprise attack or ambush.

If you choose this skill, write 'Huntmastery' on your *Action Chart*.

Pathsmanship
In addition to the basic skill of being able to recognize the correct path in unknown territory, the Magnakai skill of Pathsmanship will enable a Kai Master to read foreign languages, decipher symbols, read footprints and tracks (even if they have been disturbed), and detect the presence of most traps. It also grants him the gift of always knowing intuitively the position of north.

If you choose this skill, write 'Pathsmanship' on your *Action Chart*.

Psi-surge
This psychic skill enables a Kai Master to attack an enemy using the force of his mind. It can be used as well as normal combat weapons and adds 4 extra points to your COMBAT SKILL.

It is a powerful Discipline, but it is also a costly one. For every round of combat in which you use Psi-surge, you must deduct 2 ENDURANCE points. A weaker form of Psi-surge called Mindblast can be used against an enemy without losing any ENDURANCE points, but it will add only 2 extra points to your COMBAT SKILL. Psi-surge cannot be used if your ENDURANCE falls to 6 points or below, and not all of the creatures encountered on your adventure will be affected by it; you will be told if a creature is immune.

If you choose this skill, write 'Psi-surge: +4 COMBAT SKILL points but −2 ENDURANCE points per round' or 'Mindblast: +2 COMBAT SKILL points' on your *Action Chart*.

Psi-screen
Many of the hostile creatures that inhabit the Darklands have the ability to attack you using their Mindforce. The Magnakai Discipline of Psi-screen prevents you from losing any ENDURANCE points when subjected to this form of attack and greatly increases your defence against supernatural illusions and hypnosis.

If you choose this skill, write 'Psi-screen: no points lost when attacked by Mindforce' on your *Action Chart*.

Nexus
Mastery of this Magnakai skill will enable you to withstand extremes of heat and cold without losing ENDURANCE points, and to move items by your powers of concentration alone.

If you choose this skill, write 'Nexus' on your *Action Chart*.

Divination

This skill may warn a Kai Master of imminent or unseen danger, or enable him to detect an invisible or hidden enemy. It may also reveal the true purpose or intent of a stranger or strange object encountered in your adventure. Divination may enable you to communicate telepathically with another person and to sense if a creature possesses psychic abilities.

If you choose this skill, write 'Divination' on your *Action Chart*.

EQUIPMENT

Before you leave Toran and begin your fateful mission, Banedon gives you a map of the Darklands (see the inside front cover of this book) and a pouch of gold. To find out how much gold is in the pouch, pick a number from the *Random Number Table*. Add 10 to the number you have picked. The total equals the number of Gold Crowns inside the pouch, and you should now enter this number in the 'Gold Crowns' section of your *Action Chart*.

Banedon also makes available a choice of equipment to help you survive in the hostile enemy heartland. For the voyage into the cold waters of the Kaltesee, you are given special fur-lined clothing, sturdy boots, and a hooded cape made from waterproof Kalkoth hide. You may also take six items from the following list, to add to any you may already possess. However, remember that you can carry a maximum of two Weapons and eight Backpack Items.

SWORD (Weapons)

BOW (Weapons)

QUIVER (Special Items) This contains six arrows. Tick them off as they are used.

ROPE (Backpack Items)

POTION OF LAUMSPUR (Backpack Items) This potion restores 4 ENDURANCE points to your total when swallowed after combat. There is enough for only one dose.

LANTERN (Backpack Items)

MACE (Weapons)

4 MEALS (Meals) Each Meal takes up one space in your Backpack.

DAGGER (Weapons)

QUARTERSTAFF (Weapons)

AXE (Weapons)

List the six items that you choose on your *Action Chart*, under the heading given in brackets, and make a note of any effect they may have on your ENDURANCE points or COMBAT SKILL.

How to carry equipment

Now that you have your equipment, refer to the list below to see how it is carried. You do not need to make notes but you can refer back to this list, if necessary, in the course of your adventure.

SWORD – carried in the hand.
BOW – carried in the hand.
QUIVER – slung over your shoulder.
ROPE – carried in the Backpack.
POTION OF LAUMSPUR – carried in the Backpack.

LANTERN — carried in the Backpack.
MACE — carried in the hand.
MEALS — carried in the Backpack.
DAGGER — carried in the hand.
QUARTERSTAFF — carried in the hand.
AXE — carried in the hand.

How much can you carry?

Weapons
The maximum number of weapons that you may carry is *two*.

Backpack Items
These must be stored in your Backpack. Because space is limited, you may keep a maximum of only eight articles, including Meals, in your Backpack at any one time.

Special Items
Special Items are not carried in the Backpack. When you discover a Special Item, you will be told how to carry it.

The maximum number of Special Items that can be carried on any adventure is twelve.

Gold Crowns
These are always carried in the Belt Pouch. It will hold a maximum of fifty Crowns.

Food
Food is carried in your Backpack. Each Meal counts as one item.

Any item that may be of use and can be picked up on your adventure and entered on your *Action Chart* is given initial capitals (eg Gold Dagger, Magic Pendant) in the text. Unless you are told it is a Special Item, carry it in your Backpack.

How to use your equipment

Weapons
Weapons aid you in combat. If you have the Magnakai Discipline of Weaponmastery and a correct weapon, it adds 3 points to your COMBAT SKILL. If you enter a combat with no weapons, deduct 4 points from your COMBAT SKILL and fight with your bare hands. If you find a weapon during the adventure, you may pick it up and use it. (Remember that you can only carry *two* weapons at once.)

Bow and Arrows
During your adventure there will be opportunities to use a bow and arrow. If you equip yourself with this weapon, and you possess at least one arrow, you may use it when the text of a particular section allows you to do so. The bow is a useful weapon for it enables you to hit an enemy at a distance. However, a bow cannot be used in hand-to-hand combat, therefore it is strongly recommended that you also equip yourself with a close combat weapon, such as a sword or mace.

In order to use a bow you must possess a quiver and at least one arrow. Each time the bow is used, erase an arrow from your *Action Chart*. A bow cannot, of course, be used if you exhaust your supply of arrows, but the opportunity may arise during your adventure for you to replenish your stock of arrows.

If you have the Magnakai Discipline of Weaponmastery with a bow, you may add 3 to any number that you pick from the *Random Number Table*, when using the bow. If you enter combat armed only with a bow, you must deduct 4 points from your COMBAT SKILL and fight with your bare hands.

Backpack Items
During your travels you will discover various useful items which you may wish to keep. (Remember that you can only carry a maximum of eight items in your Backpack at any time.) You may exchange or discard them at any point when you are not involved in combat.

Special Items
Special Items are not carried in the Backpack. When you discover a Special Item, you will be told how to carry it.

The maximum number of Special Items that a Kai Master can carry during an adventure is twelve. Surplus Special Items may be left in safe-keeping with Banedon at Toran.

Food
You will need to eat regularly during your adventure. If you do not have any food when you are instructed to eat a Meal, you will lose 3 ENDURANCE points. If you have chosen the Magnakai Discipline of Huntmastery as one of your skills, you will not need to tick off a Meal when instructed to eat.

Potion of Laumspur
This is a healing potion that can restore 4 ENDURANCE points to your total when swallowed after combat. There is enough for one dose only. If you discover any other potion during the adventure, you will be informed of its effect. All potions are Backpack Items.

RULES FOR COMBAT

There will be occasions during your adventure when you have to fight an enemy. The enemy's COMBAT SKILL and ENDURANCE points are given in the text. Lone Wolf's aim in the combat is to kill the enemy by reducing his ENDURANCE points to zero while losing as few ENDURANCE points as possible himself.

At the start of a combat, enter Lone Wolf's and the enemy's ENDURANCE points in the appropriate boxes on the Combat Record section of your *Action Chart*.

The sequence for combat is as follows:

1. Add any extra points gained through your Magnakai Disciplines and Special Items to your current COMBAT SKILL total.

2. Subtract the COMBAT SKILL of your enemy from this total. The result is your *Combat Ratio*. Enter it on the *Action Chart*.

Example
Lone Wolf (COMBAT SKILL 15) is attacked by a Nightstalker (COMBAT SKILL 22). He is not given the opportunity to evade combat, but must stand

and fight as the creature leaps on him. Lone Wolf has the Magnakai Discipline of Psi-surge to which the Nightstalker is not immune, so Lone Wolf adds 4 points to his COMBAT SKILL, giving him a total COMBAT SKILL of 19.

He subtracts the Nightstalker's COMBAT SKILL from his own, giving a *Combat Ratio* of −3. (19 − 22 = −3). −3 is noted on the *Action Chart* as the *Combat Ratio*.

3. When you have your *Combat Ratio*, pick a number from the *Random Number Table*.

4. Turn to the *Combat Results Table* on the inside back cover of the book. Along the top of the chart are shown the *Combat Ratio* numbers. Find the number that is the same as your *Combat Ratio* and cross-reference it with the random number that you have picked (the random numbers appear on the side of the chart). You now have the number of ENDURANCE points lost by both Lone Wolf and his enemy in this round of combat. (*E* represents points lost by the enemy; *LW* represents points lost by Lone Wolf.)

Example

The *Combat Ratio* between Lone Wolf and the Nightstalker has been established as −3. If the number picked from the *Random Number Table* is a 6, then the result of the first round of combat is:

Lone Wolf loses 3 ENDURANCE points (plus an additional 2 points for using Psi-surge).
Nightstalker loses 6 ENDURANCE points.

5. On the *Action Chart*, mark the changes in EN-DURANCE points to the participants in the combat.

6. Unless otherwise instructed, or unless you have an option to evade, the next round of combat now starts.

7. Repeat the sequence from Stage 3.

This process of combat continues until the EN-DURANCE points of either the enemy or Lone Wolf are reduced to zero, at which point the one with the zero score is declared dead. If Lone Wolf is dead, the adventure is over. If the enemy is dead, Lone Wolf proceeds but with his ENDURANCE points reduced.

A summary of Combat Rules appears on the page after the *Random Number Table*.

Evasion of combat

During your adventure you may be given the chance to evade combat. If you have already engaged in a round of combat and decide to evade, calculate the combat for that round in the usual manner. All points lost by the enemy as a result of that round are ignored, and you make your escape. Only Lone Wolf may lose ENDURANCE points during that round, but then that is the risk of running away! You may evade only if the text of the particular section allows you to do so.

LEVELS OF MAGNAKAI TRAINING

The following table is a guide to the rank and titles that are achieved by Kai Masters at each stage of their training. As you successfully complete each adventure in the Lone Wolf Magnakai series, you will gain an additional Magnakai Discipline and progress towards the ultimate distinction of a Kai Warrior – Kai Grand Mastership.

No. of Magnakai Disciplines mastered by Kai Master	Magnakai Rank
1	Kai Master
2	Kai Master Senior
3	Kai Master Superior – *You begin the Lone Wolf Magnakai adventures with this level of training*
4	Primate
5	Tutelary
6	Principalin
7	Mentora
8	Scion-kai
9	Archmaster
10	Kai Grand Master

LORE-CIRCLES OF THE MAGNAKAI

In the years before their massacre, the Kai Masters of Sommerlund devoted themselves to the study of the Magnakai. These skills were divided into four schools of training called 'Lore-circles'. By mastering all of the Magnakai Disciplines of a Lore-circle, the Kai Masters developed their fighting prowess (COMBAT SKILL), and their physical and mental stamina (ENDURANCE) to a level far higher than any mortal warrior could otherwise attain.

Listed below are the four Lore-circles of the Magnakai and the skills that must be mastered in order to complete them.

Title of Magnakai Lore-circle	Magnakai Disciplines needed to complete the Lore-circle
CIRCLE OF FIRE	Weaponmastery & Huntmastery
CIRCLE OF LIGHT	Animal control & Curing
CIRCLE OF SOLARIS	Invisibility, Huntmastery & Pathsmanship
CIRCLE OF THE SPIRIT	Psi-surge, Psi-shield, Nexus & Divination

By completing a Lore-circle, you may add to your COMBAT SKILL and ENDURANCE the extra bonus points that are shown below.

Lore-circle bonuses

	COMBAT SKILL	ENDURANCE
CIRCLE OF FIRE	+1	+2
CIRCLE OF LIGHT	0	+3
CIRCLE OF SOLARIS	+1	+3
CIRCLE OF THE SPIRIT	+3	+3

All bonus points that you acquire by completing a Lore-circle are additions to your basic COMBAT SKILL and ENDURANCE scores.

IMPROVED DISCIPLINES

As you rise through the higher levels of Magnakai training you will find that your skills will steadily improve. If you are a Kai Master who has reached the rank of Primate (four skills), Tutelary (five skills), Principalin (six skills), Mentora (seven skills), Scion-kai (eight skills), or Archmaster (nine skills), you will now benefit from the improvements to the following Magnakai Disciplines:

PRIMATE

Animal Control
Primates with this Magnakai Discipline are able to repel an animal that is intent on harming them by blocking its sense of taste and smell. The level of success is dependent on the size and ferocity of the animal.

Curing
Primates with this skill have the ability to delay the effect of any poisons, including venoms, that they may come into contact with. Although a Kai Primate with this skill is not able to neutralize a poison, he is able to slow its effect, giving him more time to find an antidote or cure.

Huntmastery
Primates with this skill have greatly increased agility and are able to climb without the use of climbing aids, such as ropes, etc.

Psi-surge
Primates with the Magnakai Discipline of Psi-surge can, by concentrating their psychic powers upon an object, set up vibrations that may lead to the disruption or destruction of the object.

Nexus
Primates with the skill of Nexus are able to offer a far greater resistance than before to the effects of noxious gases and fumes.

TUTELARY

Weaponmastery

Tutelaries are able to use defensive combat skills to great effect when fighting unarmed. When entering combat without a weapon, Tutelaries lose only 2 points from their COMBAT SKILL, instead of 4 points.

Invisibility

Tutelaries are able to increase the effectiveness of their skill when hiding from an enemy by drawing the enemy's attention to a place other than that in which they are hiding. The effectiveness of this ability increases as a Kai Master rises in rank.

Pathsmanship

Tutelaries with this skill can detect an enemy ambush within 500 yards of their position unless their ENDURANCE level is low due to a large number of wounds sustained or to lack of food.

Psi-screen

Tutelaries with this skill develop mental defences against magical charms and hostile telepathy. The effectiveness of this ability increases in strength as a Kai Master rises in rank.

Divination

Tutelaries who possess this Magnakai Discipline are able to recognize objects or creatures with magical skills or abilities. However, this improved Discipline can be negated if the creature or object is shielded from detection.

PRINCIPALIN

Animal Control
Principalins with this skill are able to call on a woodland animal (if nearby) to aid them, either in combat, or to act as a messenger or guide. The number of animals that can be summoned increases as a Kai Master rises in rank.

Invisibility
Principalins are able to mask any sounds made by their movements while using this skill.

Huntmastery
Principalins with this Magnakai Discipline are able to intensify their eyesight at will, giving them telescopic vision.

Psi-surge
Principalins using this skill in combat are able to confuse an enemy by planting seeds of doubt in its mind. The effectiveness of this ability increases as a Kai Master rises in rank.

Nexus
Principalins with this ability can extinguish fires by force of will alone. The size of the fire, and the number that can be extinguished using Nexus increases as a Kai Master rises in rank.

MENTORA

Weaponmastery
Mentoras skilled in Weaponmastery are more accurate when using all missile weapons, whether fired (eg, a bow) or thrown (eg, a dagger). When using a bow or thrown weapon and instructed to pick a number from

the *Random Number Table*, add 2 to the number picked if you are Mentora with the Magnakai Discipline of Weaponmastery.

Curing
Mentoras with this skill are able to neutralize the effects of any poisons, venoms or toxins with which they come into contact.

Pathsmanship
Mentoras who possess this Magnakai Discipline are able to cross any kind of terrain on foot without leaving any tracks, even if the ground is covered in snow.

Psi-screen
Mentoras with this ability can protect themselves from evil spirits, and any other non-corporeal beings, that attack using psychic energy. The effectiveness of this ability increases as a Kai Master rises in rank.

Divination
Mentoras who possess this skill are able to detect psychic residues lingering in a place where a dramatic event, such as a battle, a murder, a ritual sacrifice or a ritual ceremony, has taken place. By meditating at the scene of the incident, a Kai Mentora is able to visualize the event, even though it may have occurred in the far distant past.

SCION-KAI

Weaponmastery
When entering combat with a weapon they have mastered, Scion-kai may add 4 points (instead of the usual 3 points) to their COMBAT SKILL. Also, when in combat without a weapon they lose only 1 point from their COMBAT SKILL.

Invisibility

Scion-kai are able to alter their physical appearance at will in order to deceive an enemy. The duration and effectiveness of this deception increases as a Kai Master rises in rank.

Pathsmanship

Scion-kai with this ability are able to converse with any sentient creature. They are also able to make themselves invisible when subjected to any psychic or magical spells of detection.

Psi-screen

When engaging in psychic combat, Scion-kai are able to absorb and control some of the energies directed at them. By deflecting or inducing the hostile energy they can either reduce the damage they sustain, or increase the power of their own psychic attacks.

Divination

Scion-kai are able to leave their body in a state of suspended animation and, in spirit form, explore their immediate surroundings unhindered by physical limitations. This ability is called 'spirit walking'. The length of time a Kai Master can spirit walk increases as he rises in rank. When the spirit is separated from the body in this fashion, the body remains inanimate and vulnerable to attack. If a Kai Master's body is killed whilst he is spirit walking, his spiritual self will also cease to exist, and vice versa.

ARCHMASTER

Animal Control

Archmasters with this skill are able to command most animals to do their bidding, although effectiveness is diminished when attempting to control a hostile creature.

Curing

Archmasters are able to use their healing power to repair serious wounds sustained in battle. If, whilst in combat, their COMBAT SKILL is reduced to 6 points or less, they can use their skill to restore 20 ENDURANCE points. This ability can only be used once every 100 days.

Huntmastery

Archmasters who possess this ability benefit from greatly increased senses of hearing, smell, and night vision. These senses become even more acute upon attaining the rank of Kai Grand Master.

Psi-surge

When using their psychic ability to attack an enemy, Archmasters may add 6 points to their COMBAT SKILL instead of the usual 4 points. For every round in which Psi-surge is used, Archmasters need only deduct 1 ENDURANCE point. When using the weaker psychic attack – Mindblast – they may add 3 points without loss of ENDURANCE points. Archmasters cannot use Psi-surge if their ENDURANCE score falls to 4 points or below.

Nexus

Archmasters with the skill of Nexus are able to withstand extremes of heat and cold, and possess limited immunity to harmful elements, such as flames, toxic gases, and corrosive liquids. The duration of this immunity increases greatly upon attaining Kai Grand Mastership.

MAGNAKAI WISDOM

Your mission to destroy Darklord Gnaag will be fraught with awesome dangers. Be secretive and be on your guard at all times, for the creatures of the Darklands will stop at nothing to destroy you should your return to Magnamund become known to them.

Some of the things that you will find during your mission will be of use to you, and some may be red herrings of no real value at all, so be selective in what you decide to keep.

If this is your first *Lone Wolf* adventure, be sure to choose your three Magnakai Disciplines with care, for a wise choice will enable any player to complete the mission, no matter how weak their initial COMBAT SKILL and ENDURANCE points scores. Successful completion of previous *Lone Wolf* adventures, although a considerable advantage, is not essential for the completion of this adventure.

At last the chance to avenge the massacre of the Kai is within your grasp. The restoration of your warrior brotherhood and the future of Magnamund depend on your success. May the spirit of your ancestors and the wisdom of the great god Kai guide you to victory and the fulfilment of your destiny.

1

Upon entering the Shadow Gate you are submerged in total darkness and fall into a lightless void. Relentlessly you are buffeted and numbed by an intense coldness that drains the strength from your body and fills your mind with strange, dream-like images. It is as if you are being sucked into the heart of a swirling black abyss, and, as your senses fade, you pray that you have enough strength to survive your return to Magnamund.

Barely a flicker of consciousness remains when the sensation of warmth returns to your frozen limbs. It revives you and slowly you become aware of a fluorescent mist and a pinpoint of light in the far distance. The sensation of falling is replaced by a smooth forward movement, as if you are gliding to a halt at the end of a steep slide. Rapidly the tiny light grows larger until suddenly you emerge from the darkness and find yourself standing in a place that you recognize immediately.

Pick a number from the *Random Number Table* (if you pick a *0* it counts as 10). The number you have picked represents the number of ENDURANCE points you have lost during your passage through the Shadow Gate. Deduct this number of points from your ENDURANCE score.

Turn to **94**.

2

You unsheathe your weapon and brace yourself to avoid the creature's leap. It springs forward and you roll aside, striking upwards as it blocks out the light. It shrieks as your blow tears deep into its shoulder, then it hits the ground, which shudders beneath the vast stone weight. You jump to your feet and prepare to strike another blow as the creature, squealing pitifully from the pain of its wound, draws itself up and leaps again.

Egorgh: COMBAT SKILL 22   ENDURANCE 27

This creature is particularly susceptible to psychic attack; double all bonuses you would normally be entitled to if using Mindblast or Psi-surge during the combat.

If you win the combat, turn to **153**.

3

You unsheathe a weapon and attempt to parry Gnaag's sword, but the supernatural blade shears straight through it and buries itself deep in your chest. An icy chill engulfs your body and you feel your chest constrict as Gnaag withdraws his hellblade. Darkness engulfs your vision and your ears are filled with a ghastly sound – the mocking laughter of Darklord Gnaag. He raises his infernal sword, Nadazgada, and prepares to deliver the blow that will seal your doom and destroy the hopes of those who oppose the empire of the Darklands.

Your life and your mission end here.

4

Your senses tingle: someone is about to attack you from behind. Without turning to see who is approaching, you twist aside, and your would-be attacker crashes chest-first against the rail. He is a Drakkarim marine armed with a stiletto dagger, whose needle-thin blade glows wetly crimson in the flickering light of the fire. Maddened by the pain of the fearful burns he has sustained on his face and hands, he screams a curse and leaps at you wildly, determined to drive his dagger into your chest.

Drakkarim Marine:
COMBAT SKILL 19   ENDURANCE 23

Owing to the frenzy of his attack, he is immune to Mindblast (but not Psi-surge).

You can evade combat after two rounds by leaping into the sea: turn to **58**.

If you win the combat, turn to **91**.

5

Your adversary is little more than a few feet away when you release your bow string to send an arrow streaking towards his chest. It hits with terrific force but, to your utter amazement, it fails to penetrate his flesh; the shaft shatters into a dozen harmless shards. With a scream of gleeful vengeance, the Drakkar officer swings his scimitar down to cleave your neck in two. Instinct alone saves you from its razor-sharp edge. Immediately, he strikes again, swinging his blade back in a vicious arc that is aimed at your throat. You block the blow but it costs you your bow, chopped almost in half as it stops the blade barely inches from your chin (remember to delete this weapon from your Weapons list). Hurriedly you fumble for a hand weapon as he steadies himself to strike again.

Drakkar Marine Officer:
COMBAT SKILL 27   ENDURANCE 38

You are unable to draw a weapon until the beginning of the second round of the combat, and must fight the first round unarmed.

If you win, and the fight lasts three rounds or less, turn to **232**.

If you win, and the fight lasts longer than four rounds, turn to **148**.

6

As you sunder the last of the Crypt Spawn, Kraagenskûl reaches out to touch the surface of a bowl that rests on a plinth beside his throne. It is filled with a bright, silvery liquid and at once you sense its purpose. It is a communicator, a device that enables him to speak with his leader, Darklord Gnaag. The Sommerswerd had betrayed your identity and Kraagenskûl is about to warn his master that you have returned from the Daziarn and are here in Argazad. As his bony fingers dip to within inches of the shimmering surface, your only hope of stopping him is to hurl the Sommerswerd at his back.

Pick a number from the *Random Number Table*. If you have completed the Lore-circle of Solaris, add 2 to the number you have picked. If you have completed the Lore-circle of Solaris *and* the Lore-circle of Fire, add another 1 to the number.

If your total is now *0–5*, turn to **275**.

If it is 6 or more, turn to **75**.

7 — *Illustration I (overleaf)*

You pull away from your adversary and retreat towards the middle of the ship. There, a group of Kirlundins have drawn up in a circle and are holding their ground behind a wall of shields. You join them and take command as a second wave of Drakkarim clamber over the side and come howling across the deck. With a noise like thunder they fall upon the group, their swords and axes drawing sparks as they rain down upon the shield-wall with numbing force. The shock of their impact drives the Kirlundins back, opening gaps in their defence through which the strongest Drakkarim hurl themselves recklessly. One breaks through close to where you stand and stabs at your neck with his blunted sword.

Drakkar Marine: COMBAT SKILL 23   ENDURANCE 27

Owing to his state of battle-frenzy, this foe is immune to Mindblast (but not Psi-surge).

If you win the combat, turn to **294**.

8

'Ok zee okak!' whispers a Giak scout, a sneer spreading slowly across his ugly grey face. He has scrambled on to a boulder and, using his infra-vision (the ability to see warm objects radiating in the dark), he has caught sight of you crawling towards the cliffs. Your sixth sense informs you that you have been spotted. To continue to crawl is futile, so you scramble to your feet and sprint towards a V-shaped cleft that marks the start of a steep trail. You have taken less than a dozen

I. A Drakkar Marine stabs at your neck with his sword

strides when three squat shapes loom out of the shadows ahead: they are Giaks, armed and ready for combat.

Giaks: COMBAT SKILL 19   ENDURANCE 27

Unless you have the Magnakai Discipline of Huntmastery or Divination, deduct 2 points from your COMBAT SKILL for the first two rounds of the fight.

> If you win and the fight lasts three rounds or less, turn to **311**.
> If you win, and the fight lasts four rounds or more, turn to **252**.

9

You dive aside, but you are hit by the whirring tip of the sword, which slices through your cape and lays open your shoulder: lose 3 ENDURANCE points.

Gritting your teeth against the sharp pain, you grab the rear of the cannon and revolve it on its mounting until it points directly at the advancing Drakkarim marines. Their faces freeze with terror when they find themselves staring into the muzzle of their own formidable weapon. 'Death to the Darklords!' you cry, and pull the firing lever.

Turn to **285**.

10

The day is but an hour old when suddenly it begins to get darker. A ceiling of black cloud spreads across the sky, fed by billowing plumes of noxious gases that pour from the cracks and craters of the southern wastes. Violent electrical storms rage in these plumes and a thunderous rumbling, like the growling of an angry giant disturbed from sleep, echoes in the bowels of the lifeless earth.

A redness in the clouds grows stronger as the Zlanbeast flies westwards. It fills the horizon, setting your pulse racing as you sense that Nengud-kor-Adez, the chasm of fire that surrounds Helgedad, is the source of the scarlet glow. You correct your course, steering the Zlanbeast away to the north, and within minutes you catch your first glimpse of Aarnak.

It is a grim spectacle, a mass of huge steel buildings grouped haphazardly around the mouth of a frigid estuary, surrounded in turn by a defensive ring of spike-topped earthworks. Everything appears to be eaten by rust, aggravated by clouds of corrosive steam that arise from rivulets of black water criss-crossing the ground. It strikes you as an uninhabitable place, yet its murky throughfares are teeming with thousands of grey-skinned creatures, all pulling or pushing great iron carts filled with ore. As the Zlanbeast speeds towards the city, you search for somewhere suitable to land.

> If you possess the Magnakai Discipline of Hunt-mastery, and have reached the Kai rank of Principalin or more, turn to **127**.
> If you do not possess this skill, or have yet to reach this level of Kai training, turn to **301**.

11

Using your Kai skill, you will the Zlanbeast to cease its incessant caw. Immediately it obeys your psychic command and shuffles to the end of its perch, its head bowed and its eyes half-closed. The Death Knight starts to turn away from the parapet, but his movements are slow and relaxed, and he is totally unprepared to receive your attack. Like a striking viper you lash out at his chest with deadly effect.

Turn to **139**.

12

The great sea beast roars, and a blast of putrid breath blows you away from the longboat, rolling you over and over like a leaf in a storm. Pain lances through your shoulder as you glance off the main mast and crash against the ship's starboard rail: lose 2 ENDURANCE points.

Your bow is still gripped firmly in your hand, and, as you struggle to your feet, you draw a fresh arrow and take aim once more at the monster's head.

If you wish to fire at the creature's eye, turn to **82**.
If you wish to fire into the creature's mouth, turn to **236**.
If you decide to fire at the creature's ear, turn to **135**.

13

Desperately, you draw on your inner strength to fight the poison that is coursing through your veins. Your Kai skill of Curing blocks the deadly effects of this viral poison, and quickly eradicates it from your system, but at a loss of 5 ENDURANCE points.

Gritting your teeth against the pain, you wrench the evil shaft from your shoulder and cast it aside as you run for the safety of the shadows.

Turn to **48**.

14

The tide bears you swiftly towards a shingle beach, which is littered with huge, sea-smoothed boulders. The hissing surf and the screech of the loathsome sea-scavengers echo all along this barren coastline. It is an unwelcoming sound − cold and hostile − a fitting reflection of the land itself.

Ten yards from the stony beach you slip into the thigh-deep foam and wade ashore. Night has fallen swiftly, but there is a full moon by which to see. It pierces the darkness and bathes the landscape in its ghostly ashen light. Crouching low, you scurry up the beach, using the boulders as cover as you head towards the base of a sheer cliff wall. You are nearing your goal when the sounds of footsteps and gruff voices stop you dead in your tracks: it is a patrol of Giak soldiers. Drawn from their cliff-top encampment, having witnessed the battle at sea, they are searching the water's edge for survivors. The tips of their spears glint wetly crimson in the moonlight, alerting you to the fate that has befallen those of Davan's crew who managed to swim ashore.

'Ok zee orgadak!' growls one of the leading scouts, pointing in your direction.

> If you have the Magnakai Discipline of Invisibility, and have reached the Kai rank of Tutelary or more, turn to **215**.
> If you do not possess this skill, or have yet to reach this level of Kai training, turn to **111**.

15

You are in combat with an alert Vladoka − an elite

Nadziranim temple guard. You cannot evade this combat and must fight your adversary to the death.

Vladoka: COMBAT SKILL 28   ENDURANCE 35

Owing to the power of the weapon he wields, this being is immune to Mindblast and Psi-surge.

If you win the combat, turn to **308**.

16

You are expecting the sudden chill of cold water, so it comes as a great shock when you slam down upon the moving steel deck of the Darkland ironclad. Your legs buckle and your knees hit your chest, forcing the air from your lungs and leaving you gasping like a fish out of water: lose 3 ENDURANCE points. You have barely recovered when a Drakkar sailor, armed with a billhook, looms out of the smoke and lunges at your head.

Drakkar Sailor: COMBAT SKILL 19   ENDURANCE 24

Unless you possess the Magnakai Discipline of Huntmastery, reduce your COMBAT SKILL by 4 points for the first two rounds of this fight, owing to the shock of your landing and the surprise of your enemy's attack.

If you win the combat, turn to **243**.

17

When you fail to answer, the burly sergeant strides forward and repeats his command impatiently. You meet his cold stare and project a surge of psychic energy directly into his brain. He begins to shiver, his cruel eyes widening as your attack erodes his ability to concentrate. You will him to allow you to pass, and mechanically he turns around to face his troops. 'Agna Tok!' he says. 'Dok lug shad.'

As the armoured soldiers stand aside, you ride quickly through the gate and along a shadowy street that leads down to the quay. At the end of the street is a sign that indicates the way to the two main areas of Argazad: the ironclad harbour and the supply depot.

If you wish to investigate the harbour, turn to **295**.

If you wish to investigate the supply depot, turn to **328**.

18

Despite your fatigue, you will yourself to stay awake and watchful. The hours crawl by but your caution finally pays off when, at the height of the storm, a hulking shape appears at the entrance, its shaggy bulk silhouetted by the constant lightning. Sensing your presence in its lair, the creature emits a hungry growl and gets ready to leap at your chest.

If you have a bow and wish to use it, turn to **264**.

If you do not, turn to **2**.

19

As the name leaves your lips, the tip of the crystal shard glows bright amber. Instantly the guard reaches for a lever in the wall, and before you can prevent him, he pulls it, setting an alarm bell clanging. In a matter of seconds, the courtyard is awash with a nightmare legion of snarling, screaming, snapping horrors. They fall upon you, and although you slay many, they overpower you eventually and haul you in chains before Darklord Gnaag. With cruel glee, he orders you to be cast into the Lake of Blood, where your endless suffering will feed its unholy flames for all eternity.

Tragically, on the threshold of victory, your natural life and mission end here.

20

You throw yourself to the deck as the missile drops like a meteor from the sky. It passes overhead, between the main and mizzen masts, then hits the water with a tremendous splash. The other enemy vessels start to turn to bring their weapons to bear, but the heavy iron ships are slow and cumbersome, and by the time they have altered position, the *Intrepid* is out of range and sailing at speed into the dully gleaming waters of the Kaltesee.

Turn to **71**.

21

Desperately you draw on your psychic defences, erecting a shield to deflect the surge of mental energy that is coursing through your mind.

Pick a number from the *Random Number Table*. For every Magnakai Discipline you possess, including your initial three skills, add 1 to the number you have picked.

If your total is now *0–6*, turn to **244**.
If it is 7 or more, turn to **152**.

22

You are pulling yourself over the parapet when the silence is shattered by the piercing clang of a bell.

23

'Ok zee orgadak iak zordak tozaz!' screams a Giak sentry, leaning out of the watchtower window. With one hand he is pointing at you with a sword and with the other he is tugging frantically at the cord of an alarm bell. You curse your luck as you turn to face the two sentries who are now rushing along the battlements, their spears held ready to stab you to death.

Giak Sentries: COMBAT SKILL 17   ENDURANCE 22

> You can evade combat at any time by leaping from the battlements to the ground below, a jump of over twenty feet: turn to **96**.
> If you possess the Sommerswerd, and wish to use it, turn to **247**.
> If you win the combat, turn to **349**.

23 – *Illustration II*

Your lightning-fast reflexes save you from the small, jelly-like creature that is plummeting towards your head. You sidestep and it hits the floor with a splat like a handful of falling mud. Immediately it springs towards your face, forcing you to defend yourself as best you can.

Plaak: COMBAT SKILL 30   ENDURANCE 10

This creature is immune to Mindblast and Psi-surge. Owing to the speed of its attack, unless you possess the Magnakai Discipline of Huntmastery, you are unable to draw a weapon and must fight the first round of combat unarmed.

> If you win the combat, turn to **312**.

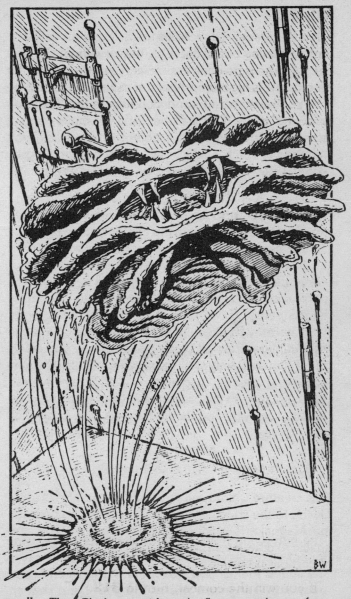

II. The Plaak springs from the floor towards your face

24

The mate leads you through the bowels of the ship to your quarters near the stern. You are hoping for some degree of comfort but the cabin turns out to be cramped and smelly, sandwiched between the galley and the bilge. Despite the lack of space, and a stomach-churning smell redolent of dead fish, you manage to catch a few hours' sleep before the grey dawn haze filters through the glass of the cabin's solitary porthole.

Desperate for fresh air, you make your way up to the forecastle where you find the captain, standing alone at the rail, reading the contents of the envelope. ' 'Tis a brave risky adventure you've committed yourself to, comrade,' he says, without raising his eyes from the parchment clutched in his gloved hands. 'Yet these be risky times. I can only guess at what lies beyond your journey to Dejkaata, but of one thing you can be sure — I will do all in my power to see you safely there.' Immediately, he issues orders to turn the ship about and steer a new course — north-by-north west. The crew react to the sudden change of plan with great speculation, yet, despite the dangers they know they may have to face, none challenge their captain's decision or voice dissent.

Turn to **241**.

25

The harrowing howls of your pursuers are growing louder with each passing second. The ghastliness of the sound makes you shiver involuntarily and ruins your aim. The arrow misses the guard and shatters against the wall of the tower, its steel tip drawing sparks, which causes the creature to give a yell of shocked surprise. Fearful that his cry will alert those who are following you, you shoulder your bow hurriedly and draw a hand weapon. Then you sprint towards the startled guard, grimly determined to finish him before he raises the alarm.

If you possess the Sommerswerd and wish to use it to slay this creature, turn to **208**.

If you do not possess this Special Item, or do not wish to use it, turn to **15**.

26

Your Kai sense informs you that the stairs descend to the control cabin and crew's quarters then on to the cargo sections which house huge tanks filled with sulphur, used as fuel for the engine of this strange craft. The sudden appearance of the sailor's body has started a commotion, and the sound of heavy boots grating on metal warns you that more Drakkarim are ascending the stairs to investigate what, or who, caused their comrade's death. To attempt to descend the stairs could prove fatal, so hurriedly you slam shut the door and look for another place to hide.

Turn to **169**.

27

'Kuzoknar jeg okak eg?' bellows the Giak, angrily. 'Okak nenrak! Okak gaj!' He is clearly unimpressed by your demand, and, as he and his two subordinates draw their swords, you decide that the time for talk is over.

Aarnak Giaks: COMBAT SKILL 23   ENDURANCE 27

If you win the combat, turn to **322**.

28

The Drakkarim lie entangled at your feet, their heaped bodies a grim testimony to the deadly art of a Kai lord in battle. You step back from your lifeless foes, grabbing the ship's rail as the deck lists heavily to starboard. The *Intrepid* is sinking fast.

'Abandon ship!' cries Davan, his voice carrying above the clangour of striking swords and dying men. As he rushes past you, followed closely by two blood-spattered Kirlundins, he urges you to save yourself before the ship goes down.

If you wish to follow Davan, and abandon ship, turn to **110**.

If you decide to search the bodies of your dead enemies first, turn to **317**.

29

Boldly you approach the two bovine guards, confident that your disguise will deceive them into letting you pass. Using the Giak language, you request that they open the door. 'Tok etaar!' you say, in a commanding tone. The guards are unimpressed. Slowly one of them reaches to his belt pouch and removes a strange, box-shaped device fashioned from silvery crystal. He flicks it open and it emits a loud humming noise.

If you possess the Magnakai Discipline of Psi-screen, and have attained the Kai rank of Scion-kai or more, turn to **141**.

If you do not possess this skill, or have yet to reach this level of Kai training, turn to **291**.

30

Using your advanced Kai skills, you lower yourself over the edge of the path and begin a perilous descent to the beach below. Twice your fingers lose their grip, but on both occasions your reflexes save you from falling backwards to your doom. Above, you hear angry shouts as the two Giak search parties converge and discover you gone. They blame each other for allowing you to escape, and, in the ensuing scuffle, more than one screaming body falls past you to crash on the rocks below. Arrows begin to fall from the cliff's edge, but they are poorly aimed and few come within an arm's length of hitting you. Order returns and the Giaks start to descend the steep path, but by then it is too late for them to catch you, as you escape northwards along the shore.

Turn to **157**.

31

Your Kai senses warn you that if you were to invert the tube, the acceleration of power inside the orange tank would lead to an immediate and devastating explosion. Rather than risk your life and your mission by tampering with the tube, you decide instead to remove some of the fabric that insulates the cables running close to the tank. The effects of this sabotage may not be felt until the vessel has been at sea for some time, but when the cables eventually disintegrate, it will rob the juggernaut of all its power. Should this happen during one of the Kaltesee's frequent storms, then an iron-hulled craft this large would be sure to capsize and sink without trace.

Turn to **223**.

32

Drawing on your advanced Magnakai skills, you cause your facial characteristics to become harder and more brutal in appearance.

'Loga ok okak sheg!' (*Free me you dog!*) you growl in Giak, mimicking the Drakkarim accent to perfection. In the confines of the corridor, your assailant is easily deceived into thinking that he has assaulted one of his fellow marines by mistake. The moment he releases his grip, you spin around and attack with your bare but deadly hands.

Drakkar (surprise attack):
COMBAT SKILL 12   ENDURANCE 26

You must fight the first two rounds of combat

unarmed. Only at the start of the third round are you able to unsheathe a hand weapon.

If you win the combat, turn to **253**.

33

Using your advanced Kai skill, you focus your hearing on what is being said by the suspicious-looking group. To your dismay you hear them plotting to ambush and kill you. They are followers of Darklord Taktaal, arch-rival of Darklord Ghanesh, whose colours you are wearing. They plan to murder you in retaliation for the death of one of their own, who was poisoned by Ghanesh's minions.

You watch them out of the corner of your eye, and, as soon as they turn away their heads, you hurry into a tunnel that has been avoided by the other passengers. The speed of your action catches the group by surprise; none of them sees which tunnel you take and you escape with ease.

Turn to **170**.

34

Your greatly enhanced ability to see into the distance, and in the dark, enables you to recognize at once that the cave-like opening in the side of the mountain is a perfectly smooth archway. It has been carved from the rock purposefully, and is not a natural fissure or fault.

If you wish to inspect the opening more closely, turn to **143**.

If you decide instead to return to the Giak outpost and attempt to gain entry, turn to **86**.

35

You swing clear of the rigging and leap astride the Xargath's neck, but it senses your presence and twists and bucks like a wild stallion to unseat you. Grimly you cling to its scaly hide, stabbing repeatedly at its ears and spine in the hope of disabling it before it breaks free. In desperation it tries to dislodge you, using its massive foreclaws to scratch at its neck in an attempt to hook you away.

Xargath: COMBAT SKILL 10   ENDURANCE 10

This creature is immune to Mindblast (but not Psisurge).

> You can evade combat at any time by climbing the main mast and hiding in the crow's nest: turn to **277**.
> If you win the combat, turn to **66**.

36

Icy winds tear at your mask and armour as you soar thousands of feet above the southern foothills of the Gourdanak Mountain Range. Were it not for the protection of your Golden Amulet, the bitter fury of these winds would have frozen you to death within an hour of leaving Argazad, yet you feel nothing, save exhilaration and a nagging fear of what awaits you in Aarnak.

Dawn breaks during the second hour of your flight, and in its dull grey light you glimpse the landscape as it speeds past below. To the south lies the Naogizaga, a vast plain of ash and slime-filled rifts; to the north lie the snow-capped peaks of the

Gourdanak Mountains; and ahead lies an unwelcoming vista, a desolation of stunted, poisonous vegetation and hilly crags. You are tired and hungry after your perilous ordeal in Argazad, and must now eat a Meal or lose 3 ENDURANCE points.

To continue, turn to **10**.

37

Through narrowed eyes you watch as the shape draws slowly nearer. A tingle of apprehension chills your skin when you recognize it. Emerging out of the twilight gloom comes a wagon laden with barrels and boxes, drawn by six ox-like creatures. Two Giak soldiers sit on the front seat — a driver and a guard. Behind them ride four horsemen — Drakkarim escorts, judging by their size and the cut of their black leather armour. The driver cracks his whip and you notice his eyes fix on the place where you are hiding.

Pick a number from the *Random Number Table*. If you possess the Magnakai Discipline of Invisibility, add 4 to the number you have picked.

If your total score is now *0–3*, turn to **118**.
If it is 4 or more, turn to **304**.

38

With breathtaking suddenness, the pain in your shoulder melts away and you feel yourself falling into an inky black void. You fight to remain conscious, but it is a fight you cannot hope to win, for the deadly viral poison has worked its way into your heart and its insidious effect has committed you to an everlasting sleep.

Tragically, your life and your mission end here on the streets of Helgedad.

39

You brace yourself to receive the enemy as they swarm around you, howling with primal fury, their teeth bared and their faces contorted with rage. The Drakkar officer screams, 'Darg!' and they hurl themselves recklessly upon you.

Drakkarim Assault Squad:
COMBAT SKILL 33   ENDURANCE 48

If you win the combat, turn to **28**.

40

The Black Cube is a Nadziranim power crystal, a deadly explosive charge devised by the Darkland sorcerers. Since you picked it up, the cube has become increasingly unstable, and now, as you take your first steps into the Imperial Armoury, it explodes with devastating effect. The blast triggers the Crystal Explosive that you had intended to use to destroy the Transfusor, and, in the resulting explosion, you, and this entire section of Helgedad, are blown to smithereens.

Your life and your mission end here.

41

The first mate, whose name is Davan, helps you to splint the captain's broken legs and construct a makeshift stretcher on which to carry him to his cabin. Having done what you can to make the captain comfortable, you return on deck to survey the damage.

Over half the crew have been killed or injured in the attack, and the ship itself is badly mauled. The main mast is down, the sails are shredded, and there is a gaping hole that stretches along the port beam to within a few feet of the waterline.

'We can patch up the sails and work the ship on a skeleton crew,' says Davan, peering over the shattered rail, 'but if we catch a storm this far out to sea, we're done for.'

Turn to **330**.

42

A section of the boomsail strikes your face, opening a nasty gash across your forehead: lose 4 ENDURANCE points. Stunned by the blow, you react sluggishly to the burning canvas now draped over your body. In a matter of seconds the flames and smoke have completely engulfed you, yet your clothes do not ignite and you feel absolutely no pain, save the wound to your head. Without haste or urgency you cast the blazing sail aside and emerge unburned.

Turn to **101**.

43

The Giak snatches the coins from your hand and grunts his approval. 'Dez ar ok!' he says, and leads the way. (Delete from your *Action Chart half* of the Kika you possess.)

You follow him through a maze of garbage-choked streets, past rusting tenements and squalid huts, to an iron tower at the heart of the city. Unlike all else, this tower appears to have been unaffected by the corrosive atmosphere: its surface is dull yet free from decay. The Giak speaks with another who guards its open entrance and immediately he stands aside, allowing you to enter the tower's gloomy ground floor.

Turn to **346**.

44

You are within a few feet of the crevasse, craning your neck to see into its lightless depths, when suddenly a thin, snaky tendril rises out of the darkness and stabs at your chest. There is a flash and a terrible pain spreads through your body, radiating to your limbs and leaving you numb and nerveless: lose 6 ENDURANCE points.

If you survive the attack, turn to **55**.

45

'Orgadak dik!' growls the leading Drakkar, when first you appear before them. Then he glances at his men and hisses the command: 'Taag dok!' They leap forward and attack you simultaneously.

Drakkarim Escorts:
COMBAT SKILL 26   ENDURANCE 34

If you win the combat, turn to **182**.

46

You press yourself against the wall. Keeping to the shadows and using your camouflage expertise, you hide from the approaching Liganim.

Pick a number from the *Random Number Table*. If you possess the Magnakai Discipline of Invisibility *and* Psi-screen, add 4 to the number you have picked.

If your total is now *0–5*, turn to **348**.
If it is 6 or more, turn to **70**.

47

Your greatly improved Magnakai skill enables you to see a string of dark shapes on the distant horizon — enemy ships. The five squat, ugly-looking vessels all lack sail or masts, or any other visible forms of propulsion, yet each moves at a constant and rapid pace. Quickly you inform the captain of what you can see and urge him to change direction, for the *Intrepid* is now heading on a collision course with the vessel at the centre of the enemy line.

Pick a number from the *Random Number Table*. If you have completed the Lore-circle of the Spirit, add 3 to the number you have picked.

If your total is now *0–5*, turn to **204**.
If it is 6 or more, turn to **129**.

48

You escape from the enemy and hide in a narrow alley, where you wait in silence. When you are sure that you are not being followed, you continue through the streets of this evil metropolis.

The way ahead is lit momentarily by an exploding fireball that showers this sector of the city with a rain of sparking cinders. In the brief light of the explosion you now see that the street along which you are walking is a cul-de-sac that ends abruptly at a square tower.

A creature, its face and body enveloped in a shroud-like robe, stands guard at the entrance to this ponderous building, clutching in its vulture-like claws a stave of iron that crackles with magical blue flames.

The sound of howling screams echoes in the darkness behind you, warning you that you are being pursued. Rather than turn and face your pursuers, you decide to take refuge in the tower, but do so you must first deal with the guard.

If you have a bow, and wish to use it, turn to **324**.
If you do not, turn to **156**.

49

You aim and fire, sending your arrow clean through the breast of the first bird and clipping the wing tip of the second as it whistles skywards. It shrieks in alarm, but rather than take fright and fly away, it banks over and dives for your eyes, determined to exact its revenge for the death of its mate.

If you have at least one arrow and wish to fire at
    your feathered attacker, turn to **107**.
If you have no arrows, or if you choose to defend
    yourself with a hand weapon, turn to **268**.

50 — *Illustration III*

You spin around to see the ghastly form of Darklord Gnaag emerge from a shadowy archway, his composite eyes glittering evilly. You stiffen at his approach, your muscles locked like coiled springs. Your whole life's struggle is concentrated into this moment: at last the time has come to avenge the Kai and rid your world of these evil masters of darkness forever. You feel a

III.   The ghastly form of Darklord Gnaag emerges from a shadowy archway

transformation taking place deep within you, a growing strength and sharpness of mind. It breathes new life into your battle-weary body and fills you with the certain knowledge that your destiny is about to be fulfilled (restore your ENDURANCE score to its original level).

The chamber echoes to a loud, rasping snarl, full of anger and fear, as Gnaag becomes aware of your true identity. You move forward, confident in your strength. But before you can attack, Gnaag fades from sight and a shimmering haze rises from the floor. The mist draws into focus and an eerie cadence, like a distant scream, fills your ears.

The phantom mist crystalizes into the shape of a winged beast with glowing ghost-eyes. It opens its fang-filled mouth and your mind screams an alarm.

If you possess the Magnakai Discipline of Divination turn to **203**.

If you do not possess this skill, turn to **102**.

51

The bosun falls screaming on to the heads of the others, his heavy body dragging them down into a heap at the foot of the stairs. You take this opportunity to escape to the surface, pausing only long enough to slam shut the steel door before looking elsewhere for some place to hide.

Turn to **169**.

52

With the toe of your boot, you turn over the body of

the dead Giak and search it for any items that may be of use. You discover the following:

> SHORT SWORD
> DAGGER
> 20 KIKA (equivalent to 2 Gold Crowns)
> ROPE

If you decide to keep any of these items, remember to adjust your *Action Chart* accordingly.

Turn to **297**.

53

You raise your arm and lash out at the speeding shaft, hoping to turn it aside on the edge of your weapon, but it ricochets towards you, gouging a furrow of skin and hair from your scalp: lose 3 ENDURANCE points. The archer fires again, but this time you manage to twist aside, and the arrow thuds harmlessly into the deck. He curses and bares his teeth as he reaches for yet another arrow. But before he can fire again, his aim is spoiled by two of his comrades, who rush forwards to hack at you with axe and sword. Davan protects your back, holding off the marines who are attempting to climb the stairs. You evade the first blows of your enemies, side-stepping a lunge and ducking a wild swipe, then strike back with deadly speed and unerring accuracy. Both scream and fall simultaneously, dying with a look of surprise fixed on their cruel faces.

Turn to **209**.

54

The door is not locked, and beyond it you discover

another hall equally as impressive as the laboratory. It is the Imperial Armoury, and it is filled with row upon row of fearsome weapons.

If you possess a Black Cube, turn to **40**.
If you do not possess this item, turn to **320**.

55

Gritting your teeth against the pain, you stagger to your feet and fumble for a weapon with numbed fingers. Suddenly, a huge shape explodes from the crevasse, rising at such a speed that its features are a blur. It emits a deafening screech, then dives towards your head, its coal-black tendril whipping the air wildly as it attempts to coil it around your neck.

Ictakko: COMBAT SKILL 25   ENDURANCE 35

Unless you possess the Magnakai Discipline of Nexus and have reached the Kai rank of Archmaster, you must lose an extra 1 ENDURANCE point every time this creature inflicts a wound during the combat, owing to the numbing effect of its electrical attack.

If you win the combat, turn to **343**.

56

The screams make the guard anxious. He levels his iron stave and adopts a fighting stance in case he should need to defend himself. His eyes, like pinpoints of red fire glowing inside the hood of his robe, catch sight of you moving in the shadows, and when you strike your first blow you discover that he is poised to parry it on the shaft of his stave.

If you possess the Sommerswerd, and wish to use it, turn to **208**.

If you do not possess this Special Item, or do not wish to unsheathe it, turn to **15**.

57

You draw the sun-sword and a gout of golden flame engulfs the blade, flaring with such brilliance that you are momentarily blinded. Kraagenskûl shrieks. It is an unearthly howl, filled with blind terror. He throws up his skeletal hands to shield himself from the searing light, and smoke curls from his blistering skin as the radiant power of the Sommerswerd burns his flesh. Sparks explode as you fend off the swarming cloud of Crypt Spawn, your blade destroying them with ease, but Kraagenskûl summons yet more of the horrors, and you are hard pressed to keep from being overwhelmed.

Crypt Spawn Flood:
COMBAT SKILL 30   ENDURANCE 36

If you win, and the fight lasts three rounds or less, turn to **6**.

If you win, and the fight lasts four rounds or more, turn to **195**.

58

You hit the water with a mighty splash and sink like a stone beneath the icy waves, yet the shock serves to electrify your senses and you quickly strike out for the surface. You emerge from the depths, coughing and gasping for air, in time to see the enemy ironclad come steaming alongside the blazing *Intrepid*. Its great steel hull passes within a few yards of where you are treading water. Fearful that you could be drowned in its wake, you swim towards it and latch on to the bow as it moves past. The heads of the rivets, which secure its steel skin, offer a handhold for your fingers and enable you to drag yourself on to its deck.

You have had barely enough time to draw breath when a Drakkar sailor, armed with a billhook, rushes forwards and aims a blow at your head.

Drakkar Sailor: COMBAT SKILL 19   ENDURANCE 24

Unless you possess the Magnakai Discipline of Hunt-mastery, reduce your COMBAT SKILL by 2 points for the first round of this fight, owing to the speed and surprise of your enemy's attack.

If you win the combat, turn to **243**.

59

Swiftly you dive aside, hoping to escape from the creature's attack, but it changes direction in mid-air and strikes you on the shoulder.

Pick a number from the *Random Number Table*. If you have completed the Lore-circles of Light *and* Solaris, add 3 to the number you have picked.

If your total is now *0–4*, turn to **233**.
If it is 5 or more, turn to **205**.

60 — *Illustration IV (overleaf)*

From the crow's nest there comes a scream of abject horror. It echoes down the rigging, alerting all to a great scaly head that has broken through the surface twenty yards off the port bow. 'Xargath!' The lookout's cry is taken up by the crew as, one by one, they glimpse the fearful sight of this legendary terror of the Kaltesee.

'Ishir preserve us!' gasps Captain Borse, as the beast opens its jaws revealing the glitter of its jagged, razor-sharp fangs. For a moment he is stunned by the terrifying sight, but quickly he recovers and begins shouting urgent orders to his awe-struck crew. 'Man the balistas! Break out the billhooks! All hands stand by to defend the ship!'

The Xargath observes the commotion in silence, its hooded eyes aglow with baleful green fire as calmly it considers the moment to attack. Then, with an awful suddenness, it rises up from the sea, roaring and hissing angrily, and lunges forward. Captain Borse gives the order to fire and a volley of arrows and balista bolts sink into the monster's scaly throat. Undeterred, it presses its attack and falls upon the port beam with devastating effect. Tortured timbers bend and crack asunder. In seconds the deck is torn apart by huge claws, each as long as a mammoth's tusk. Then the cavernous, fang-filled mouth sweeps down through the fog to snap shut upon the forecastle. Screams of pain and terror fill the air as it withdraws, soaring

IV. The Xargath rises up from the sea and lunges at the ship

upward above the masts, jaws bulging with a dozen wriggling bodies. You take cover behind the ship's longboat with the captain and prepare to defend yourself as the Xargath returns for a second strike.

If you have a bow, and wish to use it, turn to **270**.

If you possess the Sommerswerd, and wish to use it, turn to **192**.

If you choose to unsheathe a hand weapon, turn to **344**.

61

You nod your willingness to bet on the fight, and the ugly Giak gives a lop-sided grin, exposing a mouthful of rotting fangs.

Firstly, decide how many Kika you wish to bet (the minimum bet is 10) on the outcome and note this figure in the margin of your *Action Chart*. Then, decide whether you wish to stake your money on the orange-skinned reptilian or the blue-skinned humanoid. If the fighter you have chosen wins the combat, you will receive winnings equal to double the amount of Kika you staked. Should your fighter lose the combat, you will lose all your stake.

If you wish to bet on the orange-skinned reptilian fighter, turn to **265**.

If you wish to bet on the blue-skinned humanoid, turn to **225**.

62

You are halfway across the gap when the thin ledge collapses beneath your feet. Desperately you claw at the sheer granite wall but your fingers cannot find purchase, and you fall backwards, toppling to your doom on the rocks far below.

Tragically, your life and your mission end here in the Durncrag Mountains.

63

The chainmail vest is crafted from a metallic mineral called kagonite. It is as light as wood, yet ten times harder than steel. The Darklords use an alloy of kagonite in the manufacture of weapons used by their troops, and it is this alloy which gives the blades of their weapons their black appearance.

Wearing this Kagonite Chainmail beneath your tunic will increase your COMBAT SKILL by 3 points and your ENDURANCE by 1 point. Because it is so light, it can be worn beneath any padded or metallic body armour you may possess.

Make the necessary adjustments to your *Action Chart*.

Turn to **188**.

64

With the speed and grace of a hunting leopard you launch yourself at the Drakkar rider. Pick a number from the *Random Number Table*. If you have the Magnakai Discipline of Huntmastery, add 3 to the number you have picked.

If your total is now *0–3*, turn to **237**.
If it is 4 or more, turn to **149**.

65

Using your Kai skill to adopt the crude mannerisms and dialect of the Drakkarim, you deliver your message to the sentinel and await his reply. You are nervous in case he sees through your charade, and while you speak you make sure that your hands do not stray too far from your weapons. But the Death Knight does not question your authenticity for a moment. Wearily he nods his head and, grumbling, descends the stairs, leaving you alone on the roof with the Zlanbeast.

Turn to **257**.

66

You strike your killing blow and leap to the deck as, with a final burst of strength, the Xargath pulls its head free of the wreckage. Its green eyes roll back in their sockets and it lets out a scream so loud that you are forced to cover your ears for fear of being permanently deafened. The scream grows louder until, with a mighty splash, the creature topples sideways and rolls off the deck into the fog-wreathed sea.

Turn to **217**.

67

A glancing blow to the side of your head is the first you know of the ambush that has been sprung by the group of creatures you saw whispering to each other in the chamber earlier. They were planning your murder, believing you to be a minion of Darklord Ghanesh — and arch-rival — because of the colour of your robe.

You stagger from the blow (lose 3 ENDURANCE points) but manage to keep your balance as you reach to unsheathe a weapon.

Minions of Taktaal:
COMBAT SKILL 28   ENDURANCE 28

If you possess the Sommerswerd, and wish to unsheathe it, turn to **208**.

If you win and the combat lasts four rounds or less, turn to **228**.

If the combat lasts longer than four rounds, turn to **121**.

68

The enemy crew scream and curse as they scramble up the ladder, the first of their number waving his sword with reckless bravado. He takes a swipe at your legs and you are forced to retreat for fear of losing a foot.

Ironclad Bosun:
COMBAT SKILL 20   ENDURANCE 26

If you are armed with any weapon other than a broadsword, a spear, or a quarterstaff, you must deduct 2 points from your COMBAT SKILL for the duration of the fight.

You can evade combat at the beginning of the second round by ascending to the deck above and slamming shut the door: turn to **169**.

If you win the fight, turn to **51**.

69

Having completed their task, the engineers pack away

their tools and climb down from the work platform that surrounds the orange tank. Patiently, you watch them leave the dry dock before climbing the platform ladder and planting your Crystal Explosive beneath the tank. You prime the device and turn to leave, taking care not to appear anxious or in a hurry, but as you reach the bottom of the ladder you are confronted by three Drakkarim guards, accompanied by a figure dressed in a hooded red robe. Your stomach churns when you glimpse his skeletal face, for the creature is not human — you are staring into the ghastly eyes of a Vordak!

The undead being begins to probe your mind with its psychic power and it shrieks in terror when it discovers who you really are. Instantly, you spring into action, drawing your weapon and striking out at them before they can do likewise. The Vordak drops with its skull shattered and a Drakkar staggers back, clutching desperately at his torn throat. The remaining two, having drawn their blades, now lunge at your chest in unison. You parry their attack with ease and send them both to their doom with one sweeping slice. With the explosive set to detonate at any minute, you run towards the exit, barging aside any who cross your path. You are within ten yards of the dock gates when an alarm bell wails and a troop of Death Knights appear in a line before you. 'Koga!' they command, and raise their spears.

At that moment there is a blinding flash of white light and suddenly everything seems to be happening in slow motion. You see the Death Knights falling backwards, their cloaks and leather armour sprouting tongues of flame. Buckled steel plates, twisted girders, and the bodies of screaming slaves cartwheel past you, trailing sparks as they tumble like fiery meteors. The heat and the shock of the explosion tears into your back and plunges you head-first into a black, unfeeling oblivion. Your act of sabotage has completely destroyed the ironclad juggernaut, and half of Argazad harbour, but it has cost you your life and sealed the doom of Magnamund.

Your life and your mission end here.

70

You bite your lip and keep deathly still as the Liganim passes within an arm's length of where you are hiding. He continues on his way without stopping, and, as soon as you sense it is safe, you breathe a sigh of relief and hurry away along the corridor.

Turn to **130**.

71

As the last of the enemy warships disappears into the dark, the crew give a rousing cheer. Once more they have risked their lives to run the blockade, and once again they live to tell the tale. The captain requests a damage report, and is relieved to hear that both his ship and crew have survived the close encounter at little cost.

Before leaving the forecastle, he reminds the lookouts to remain vigilant. Sometimes the enemy place a second line of ironclads a few miles behind the first in order to catch blockade runners that slip through. He bids you goodnight, and, as he descends the stairs to his cabin, he orders the first mate to show you to your quarters at the stern.

If you wish to accompany the first mate to your cabin, turn to **339**.

If you wish to hand the captain the envelope containing his new orders, turn to **142**.

72

Stunned and dazed by the impact, you fail to sense or see the four Giak soldiers creeping towards you, their bows drawn ready to fire. The hiss of their black arrows freezes your blood moments before the tips burrow into your chest. Pain hits you like a wave breaking against your body, but the agony soon fades and you slip swiftly into a sleep from which there will be no awakening.

Tragically, your life and your mission end here in the Durncrag Mountains.

73

A chilling numbness spreads through your body, starting at your neck and coursing rapidly to your hands and feet. You try to scream but no sound issues from your paralysed throat as your legs give way and you collapse on to the deck of your tiny cabin. You have fallen prey to the bite of a deadly Plaak, placed here by a rival Liganim in a bid to assassinate an old rival.

Tragically, your life and your mission end here.

74

From a tube-like contraption mounted behind the funnel of the ironclad there issues a flash and a puff of smoke. Moments later, a fiery ball comes hurtling towards the *Intrepid*, screeching louder than a flock of angry Kraan. It strikes amidships, causing an explosion that sends a thousand flaming shards hissing in every direction. In seconds the sails, masts and rigging are set ablaze, showering Drakkarim and crew alike with red-hot smoking cinders.

Instinctively you cover your head as part of the boom-sail lands close by. It brings with it a tangle of burning canvas that smothers you from head to foot.

If you possess the Magnakai Discipline of Nexus, and have reached the rank of Principalin or more, turn to **177**.

If you do not possess this skill, or have yet to reach this level of Kai training, pick a number from the *Random Number Table*.

If the number you have picked is *0–3*, turn to **42**.
If it is *4–6*, turn to **288**.
If it is *7–9*, turn to **332**.

75

The sun-sword spins through the air, its heavy blade pulling it slightly awry. You fear that it will miss the Darklord, yet it catches his outstretched hand and shears it off at the wrist before embedding itself in the chamber wall beyond. The evil lord screams in agony, cradling the severed stump in an attempt to staunch the flow of foul-smelling ichor. Then he shrieks maniacally and raises his sword with his remaining hand. He is badly wounded, but as he staggers forwards you sense that, so long as he wields his black sword, he is a formidable enemy.

Darklord Kraagenskûl (wounded):
COMBAT SKILL 30   ENDURANCE 29

This being is immune to Mindblast (but not Psi-surge). If you survive the first three rounds of combat, you are able to retrieve the Sommerswerd.

If you win the combat, turn to **240**.

76

The dry dock is unguarded and none of the Drakkarim appears to pay any special attention to you when you enter on horseback. You dismount and tether your horse to a post before making your way through the tangle of steel beams and plates that are strewn around the juggernaut's exposed keel. A group of slaves are at work near the stern, hoisting into position a strange spherical tank made of a sparkling orange metal. As soon as it is secured, the Drakkarim engineers begin coupling heavy springs and thick copper cables to the tank, linking it to a massive propeller at the rear of the craft.

Carefully you study the complex machinery, soon realizing that if the orange tank were destroyed, or damaged beyond repair, the vessel would be unable to propel itself. However, the shell of the tank appears to be constructed of super-hard metal, and the only way you can think of destroying it is by using your Crystal Explosive.

> If you wish to use your Crystal Explosive to destroy the giant ironclad, turn to **69**.
>
> If you choose not to use it, but decide to search instead for some other means of sabotaging the vessel, turn to **210**.

77

You draw an arrow and take aim at the Drakkar leader's chest. He laughs contemptuously at your bow, as if it were no more dangerous than a child's toy. Then he draws back his blade and takes aim at your neck.

> If you possess the Magnakai Discipline of Divination, and have reached the Kai rank of Tutelary or more, turn to **163**.
>
> If you do not possess this skill, or have yet to reach this level of training, turn to **5**.

78

As you strike the killing blow that punctures Taktaal's heart, he shrieks and convulses like a thrashing snake before collapsing at the edge of the dais. A foul black gas hisses from the gaping wound, and his body fades rapidly until all that is left is a dull grey stain on the shiny black steel floor.

'Ghanesh will be proud of you!' comes a voice from the shadows, full of malevolence. It is a sound that strikes terror in your heart, for instantly you recognize the rasping tone of your most hated foe – Darklord Gnaag, the Archlord of the Darklands.

Turn to **50**.

79

You drag the dead Drakkar behind the rocks and divest the body of its armour. Although not a perfect fit, the leather battle-jacket, leggings, and battle-mask make you look convincingly like a Drakkar warrior. Apart from the armour (which you need not record on your *Action Chart*), you discover a number of items that may be of use to you on the road ahead:

> SWORD
>
> DAGGER
>
> BOW
>
> QUIVER
>
> 4 ARROWS
>
> 30 KIKA (equivalent to 3 Gold Crowns)

If you decide to keep any of these items, remember to record them on your *Action Chart*.

The dead warrior's horse is standing nearby, pawing the ground nervously. Using your innate Kai skill of animal kinship, you succeed in claiming him and making him obey your commands. Slowly he approaches and allows you to climb into the saddle.

Once you are sure that you have control you flick your heels and head off at a canter along the trail to Argazad.

Turn to **200**.

80

The walls of the tunnel shimmer with reddish reflections, as though somewhere in its unknown depths a great fire is blazing. With the fear of being caught making your heart pound in your chest, you look around you, taking in every detail of your surroundings.

One thing you notice immediately is that the other Liganim all move with a pronounced limp. You take care to copy this strange, irregular gait in order not to attract suspicion. None appears to show you any undue interest until you reach a semi-circular chamber at the tunnel's end. There the passengers split up and enter numerous smaller passages that burrow beneath the city in all directions. One group, however, remains in the chamber. They huddle close together and whisper among themselves whilst casting glances at you.

If you possess the Magnakai Discipline of Huntmastery, and have reached the Kai rank of Archmaster, turn to **33**.

If you do not possess this skill, or have yet to reach this level of Kai training, turn to **249**.

81 – *Illustration V*

Before you stands a magnificent warrior, tall and

V. Before you stands a magnificent warrior, the Slavemaster

broad-shouldered, clad in purple satin and shiny steel mail. He holds you with his jade-green eyes and says: 'I am the Slavemaster. Remove your mask, Drakkar, and reveal your true self.'

Your Kai senses tell you that he speaks the truth: he is the Slavemaster of Aarnak, and he has recognized the words that identify you as a fellow-agent of the Elder Magi. But the many years he has spent as a servant of the Darklords has taught him to be wary of their subterfuge, and not until you remove your battle-mask and he looks upon your unmistakably Sommlending features does he accept you as genuine. 'Long have I waited for this moment,' he says, quietly. 'I know why you have come and I will help you all I can.'

'But why?' you reply, now suspicious of his true motives. 'Why do you desire to betray your masters? Have they not given you the power you crave?'

'Aye!' That they have, but at a grievous price. Since the war began, they have demanded that the foundries and ore pits of Aarnak produce ever-increasing supplies of black steel. The quotas are impossible and I fear that the day is close when I will be of no more use to them. Ultimately, the Darklords destroy everything over which they have control – cities, land, races, even their own kind. The Elder Magi have promised me sanctuary in return for my help, and help I shall, for my life is dependent on your success.' He smiles, amused by the irony of his situation, then he bids you follow him to an adjoining chamber. 'Come, you must prepare for your journey to the Black City.'

Turn to **154**.

82

Your arrow spirals towards the Xargath's eye and, to your astonishment, splinters to matchwood against its stone-hard cornea. Cursing your misfortune, you reach for a hand weapon as the creature advances unceasingly, its jaws widening as it prepares to swallow you whole.

Turn to **344**.

83

Your Kai skill and experience alert you to the threat of an imminent ambush. The group of creatures you saw whispering to each other in the chamber earlier are creeping up on you from behind, armed with an assortment of deadly weapons. You spin around to confront them as they prepare to attack, and catch all of them wrong-footed.

Minions of Taktaal:
COMBAT SKILL 24   ENDURANCE 28

Owing to the speed and surprise of your counter-attack, ignore any ENDURANCE points you may lose in the first two rounds of the combat.

If you possess the Sommerswerd, and wish to use it, turn to **208**.
If you win the combat, turn to **228**.

84

Silently you watch as the great tube is gradually lowered, by means of ratchets and gears, until it is pointing directly at the waterline of the *Intrepid*. It seems a pointless exercise: the ship is sinking so quickly that to fire upon it now would seem to be wasteful. Then suddenly you realize what the enemy captain is planning to do; the thought of it stirs you to anger.

Turn to **113**.

85

Standing in the corridor outside is a slim, small, seemingly insignificant figure, clad in a loose-fitting garment of plain emerald cloth. His pinched and pallid face is of human proportion, and, were it not for his pig-like snout and watery, colourless eyes, he could easily pass for one of your species.

'Humble greetings, Cagath,' he says, in a syrupy sweet tone that makes your flesh crawl. 'I bring the compliments of Bazdash-Vool, my worthy master. He invites you to join him in the gallery, where he is about to host an entertainment for his illustrious fellow passengers, to make their journey altogether less tiresome. Will you grace us with your presence, noble Cagath?'

If you wish to accept this creature's invitation and accompany him to the gallery, turn to **184**.
If you decide to decline the invitation, turn to **338**.

86

After spending two hours scrutinizing every move the Giak guards make, you are sure that the two patrolling the wall follow the same routine with little variation. Once every two minutes exactly, their beat brings them both to a point near the watchtower at the middle of the wall, where they turn about before starting another circuit of patrol.

You wait until one of the sentries reaches the end of the battlements — at a point where it abuts the sheer mountain wall — and when he turns to march back to the centre, you make your move. Crouching low, you scurry to the foot of the wall and begin to climb, counting every passing second as you struggle to find handholds in the darkness.

Pick a number from the *Random Number Table*. If you possess the Magnakai Discipline of Invisibility, add 2 to the number you have picked. If you possess the Magnakai Discipline of Huntmastery, and have reached the Kai rank of Primate or more, add 3.

If your total score is now *0–6*, turn to **22**.
If it is 7 or more, turn to **227**.

87

Cautiously you peer into the abyss, your weapon held ready in case another of the fearsome Ictakko should surge from the depths and attack. But in this instance your caution proves unnecessary, for your senses soon tell you that a colony of cave bats are the only creatures that now occupy the dark and silent crevasse.

With ease, you leap across the crevasse at its narrowest point and leave the cavern by the tunnel in the opposite wall. Here, too, the walls are encrusted with light-emitting bacteria, enabling you to progress quickly through a series of interconnecting halls and chambers. The cobwebbed remains of broken mining equipment litter many of these places, revealing why the Darklords constructed this labyrinth of tunnels. After an hour of exploration you find the main exit from the mine. Darkness greets your return to the surface, but your senses inform you that you have emerged in the pass that traverses the mountain range.

Turn to **137**.

88

Gnaag recoils in terror when he recognizes the weapon you wield. Fashioned in the fiery furnaces that lie buried deep in the bowels of the city, it possesses a power than can seal his doom. He retreats and you take up the attack in this momentous struggle.

Darklord Gnaag:
COMBAT SKILL 50   ENDURANCE 70

The power of the weapon you wield is greatly intensified when used within the walls of Helgedad. Owing to its increased power, add 12 to your COMBAT SKILL for the duration of the fight. Darklord Gnaag is immune to Mindblast (but not Psi-surge).

If you win the combat, turn to **350**.

89

Your senses warn you that a large section of the middle deck, severely weakened during the Xargath's attack, is now on the verge of collapsing beneath the weight of fighting men. Forewarned by your Kai skill, you shout an order to the Kirlundins to retreat towards the bow. Immediately they obey, pausing only to help those wounded who cannot move, and quickly withdraw before the renewed Drakkarim assault. Seconds later, with an ear-splitting crack, the timbers split asunder and the host of enemy troops suddenly disappear, amid screams and curses, into the bowels of the ship.

Turn to **334**.

90

Kraagenskûl's skeletal hand scoops up the sword a second before your own slaps the ground. You raise your eyes and your heart freezes with terror as the black blade whistles towards your neck. With the cruel, gloating laugh of the evil Darklord echoing in your ears, your life is brought to a swift and tragic conclusion.

Your mission ends here.

91

You pull away from your enemy as he screams and tumbles over the ship's rail. Then, as if in answer to his cry, a horn shrieks loudly. It is the ironclad; it has at last caught up and is steaming alongside the blazing *Intrepid*. Clouds of acrid yellow smoke now merge with the oily black plumes pouring from the inferno that was once the ship's hold, adding to the chaos and confusion. You pull yourself on to the rail and wait for the smoke to thin before you make your leap. Suddenly the ship lurches violently and you slip and fall feet-first into the swirling smog.

Pick a number from the *Random Number Table*.
If the number you have picked is 0–4, turn to **16**.
If it is 5–9, turn to **194**.

92

The Death Knight spins around and lowers his spear when he hears you approaching. He growls like a hungry lion then demands to know what you are doing here.

Pick a number from the *Random Number Table*. If you possess the Magnakai Dsicipline of Invisibility, add 3 to the number you have picked. If you have reached the Kai rank of Mentora or more, add another 2 points.

If your total is now 0–6, turn to **189**.
If it is 7 or more, turn to **65**.

93

You recognize the bacteria to be Gnallia, a beneficial bacillus that is acclaimed by the healers and herbalists of Durenor. Potions of Gnallia are often prescribed to prevent and cure infections of the blood. The raw bacteria are edible and, despite their awful taste, are rich in protein. There is enough here for more than 10 Meals. If you wish to keep some of this Gnallia, record it in the Meals section of your *Action Chart*. Each Meal of Gnallia will restore 2 ENDURANCE points.

Turn to **303**.

94 – *Illustration VI*

With your heart pounding in anticipation, you cast your gaze around the grey granite walls of a subterranean vault: your journey through the Shadow Gate

VI. As the two men raise their heads, you recognize
Banedon and Lord Rimoah

has returned you to the land of your birth. You are standing in the Externment Chamber, a room located deep below the Guildhall of the Crystal Star in Toran. Facing you, and illuminated by the glow of several tall candles, is a line of throne-like seats. Two men, both attired in silken robes, are seated at the centre of the row, their heads bowed and their hands clasped in silent prayer. The sound of your footsteps stirs them from their meditations and, as they raise their heads, you recognize the face of your friend, Banedon, and your tutor, Lord Rimoah, speaker for the High Council of the Elder Magi.

'The gods be praised!' breathes Rimoah, his eyes wide with astonishment. 'Skarn has returned. The prophecy is fulfilled.'

Slowly they rise and step forward to greet you, their movements hesitant and uncertain, scarcely able to believe that you are alive. Calmly you assure them that they are not dreaming, that you have indeed survived your exile to the Daziarn Plane and have returned, more determined than ever to avenge yourself upon Darklord Gnaag.

Eagerly Rimoah and Banedon listen as you recount your experiences in the Daziarn and, when you have finished, they tell you what has befallen Magnamund during your absence. Although it seemed that you spent little more than a few days in the Daziarn, more than eight years have passed since Gnaag caused you to fall into the Shadow Gate of Torgar. 'He was quick to proclaim your death,' says Banedon, unfurling a map of Northern Magnamund upon the floor of the chamber. 'The news came as a terrible blow to us all.'

Lord Rimoah kneels and points at the map, indicating the city of Torgar with the tip of a slender crystal rod. 'After your disappearance, Lord Adamas was killed, and the allied armies were quickly ejected from Torgar. Gnaag declared himself invincible, and in the wake of his victory the Darkland defeats were soon halted throughout central Magnamund. A terrible sense of hopelessness befell the allies, which was exploited to the full by the malevolent Gnaag. His sorcerers, the nadziranim, created devices they call "Tanoz-tukor" to enable each of the Darklords to survive in territories outside their accursed realm. Previously they had been unable to survive beyond the Darklands for any great length of time and, during these rare, brief excursions, their powers were greatly reduced. Now they are able to lead their armies in battle personally, and they have been eager to exercise their new-found freedom.'

'The war against the Darklords is all but lost,' continues Banedon, his eyes cast down at the map, which is covered with black markers indicating the frightening number of countries Gnaag has added to his empire. 'With the help of our allies in Durenor, Sommerlund has so far resisted his attempts at invasion, but now we find ourselves cut off from Durenor's aid by a blockade of Darklord warships. Here,' he says, pointing to the Gulf of Helgenag, 'is where Gnaag has constructed a huge naval base. It is called Argazad, and it is from here that he launches his fleet of ironclad warships to blockade our coast. The Sommlending navy is no match for these monstrous sea machines, and without the troops, food, and weapons we have been receiving by sea from Durenor, our days are numbered.'

Lord Rimoah rises to his feet and stares fixedly into your eyes. 'Your skill, bravery, and your vow to avenge the death of the Kai are the keys to our salvation. Only you, Lone Wolf, can save us now. You are our only hope in this hour of darkness.'

Turn to **166**.

95

You snatch a large ring of keys from the belt of a dead guard and unlock the steel door. Beyond it you discover a vast hall filled with row upon row of fearsome weaponry. It is the Imperial Armoury of Helgedad.

If you possess a Black Cube, turn to **40**.
If you do not possess this item, turn to **320**.

96

You hit the ground and roll forward to lessen the impact, but still the force of the landing numbs your legs and leaves you breathless. As you struggle to stand, your vision swims in and out of focus.

Pick a number from the *Random Number Table*. If you have completed the Lore-circle of Solaris *and* the Lore-circle of Light, add 3 to the number you have picked.

If your total is now 4 or less, turn to **72**.
If it is 5 or more, turn to **161**.

97

At the first opportunity, you leave the busy street and ride along a little-used alley. It leads to a large, flat-roofed warehouse, common in this section of Argazad. It is unlit and seemingly empty.

As you halt in front of its sliding steel door, you are startled by a loud screech and the flap of huge wings directly above. You look up to see a dark shape crossing the moonlit sky, and then plummet to land somewhere behind the warehouse. Intrigued by this shadowy creature, you decide to skirt around the warehouse and investigate.

Turn to **328**.

98

An icy cold spike of fear stabs your heart as you feel something wet and slippery land on top of your head.

Pick a number from the *Random Number Table*. If you have completed the Lore-circles of Light *and* Solaris, add 3 to the number you have picked.

If your total is now *0–4*, turn to **233**.
If it is 5 or more, turn to **205**.

99

Silently you draw an arrow to your lips and take aim at the Drakkar's throat, at the point where a thin strip of unprotected skin is visible between the chin-piece of his battle-mask and the top of his hardened-leather breastplate. A wound there should prove fatal and yet leave untarnished the armour that you intend to wear in order to gain entry to Argazad.

Pick a number from the *Random Number Table* and add to it any bow skill bonuses to which you are entitled.

If your total score is now *0–4*, turn to **336**.
If it is 5 or more, turn to **212**.

Almost invisible against the horizon of black cliffs and cloudy grey skies are two enemy warships, anchored a few hundred yards offshore. At first they look deserted, then the sudden clang of alarm bells and the appearance of huge clouds of yellow smoke from their funnels indicate they are manned, and they intend to give chase.

'Our only chance is to outrun them,' says Davan, his eyes narrowing as he surveys the ironclads hauling their anchors and turning about. At his command the crew spring into action, breaking their backs to coax every last knot of speed from their battered ship, but the winds are against them and the enemy, not reliant on sails for their propulsion, are soon closing the gap.

'Prepare to repel boarders!' shouts Davan, as an ironclad draws alongside. Hastily they abandon their attempt to outrun the enemy, and draw weapons in readiness to receive a unit of leather-clad Drakkarim marines who are poised to spring aboard the very moment the two vessels collide. Then, with a resounding crash, the ironclad smashes into the side of the *Intrepid* and the enemy come scrambling over the rail, screaming and howling like a pack of demons.

One of their number singles you out. He strides forward, his black blade swinging viciously as he attempts to cleave your skull in two. Owing to the speed of his attack you are unable to make use of a bow.

Drakkar Marine:
COMBAT SKILL 23   ENDURANCE 27

You can evade combat at any time: turn to **7**.
If you win the combat, turn to **248**.

101

At first you are puzzled by your new-found invulnerability, then you remember the Golden Amulet that Banedon gave you before you left Toran. Its magical powers have saved you from serious injury. Silently you give thanks to your old friend.

The explosion has caused havoc aboard the *Intrepid*. Men run howling across the decks, their clothes and hair ablaze, as the fire spreads swiftly throughout the ship. 'Save yourselves!' cries Davan. 'Abandon ship!' You reach the deck rail, and, as you look along the beam, you see scores of men – Drakkarim and Sommlending alike – hurling themselves into the cold, dark waters of the Kaltese rather than perish amid the roaring holocaust of fire.

If you possess the Magnakai Discipline of Huntmastery or Divination, turn to **4**.

If you do not possess either of these skills, turn to **224**.

102

You are in combat with a powerful spirit-creature, summoned by Darklord Gnaag from the Plain of Darkness. You fight to suppress your fear, for, by feeding upon it, the creature is growing stronger and stronger.

Mind Reaper: COMBAT SKILL 30   ENDURANCE 36

This supernatural being is especially susceptible to psychic attack. Double all bonuses you would normally receive if you choose to use either Mindblast or Psi-surge during the combat.

If you win the combat, turn to **306**.

103

With bated breath, you wait for the creature to appear, fearful yet confident that your bow skill will put paid to the hostile intentions of this malodorous cave-dweller.

The tip of a thin, snaky limb rises from the abyss and glides slowly across the ground towards your legs. Its skin is smooth and dark, like black velvet, and it moves with alarming speed. Suddenly it halts, as if sensing the danger, and draws itself up like a serpent preparing to strike.

If you wish to fire at the snaky limb, turn to **276**.
If you decide to hold your fire and wait for it to make the first move, turn to **185**.

104

The creature howls with malicious joy, and its Liganim followers add to this hellish cry with a chorus of cackling laughter as they spread out quickly to surround you. You have stumbled into a sector of Helgedad that is the domain of Darklord Taktaal, an arch-rival of Darklord Ghanesh whose colours you wear. With the thought of your slaughter fixed in their minds, the minions of Taktaal launch their attack. You cannot evade this combat and must fight them as one enemy.

Minions of Taktaal:
COMBAT SKILL 31   ENDURANCE 43

If you possess the sword Helshezag, and wish to use it, remember to add the appropriate bonuses to your COMBAT SKILL.

If you possess the Sommerswerd, and wish to use it, turn to **208**.

If you win the combat, turn to **164**.

105

Your arrow speeds towards its target and disappears. Seemingly uninjured, the Xargath draws back its head in readiness to strike, its awesome jaws poised to seal your doom. Death seems but moments away, when suddenly the creature freezes. It shudders, its green eyes rolling in their sockets, then gives vent to a scream so loud that you are forced to cover your ears for fear of being deafened. The scream grows louder until, with a mighty splash, the Xargath lurches sideways into the fog-wreathed sea.

Turn to **217**.

106

No sooner has the Xaghash crashed dead at your feet than you see yet more of its loathsome kind emerging from the surrounding towers. There is no time to search the dead body — to stay would be suicidal. Without hesitation, you turn on your heel and run for your life.

Turn to **48**.

107

The bird approaches at incredible speed, its black body difficult to make out against the darkening cloud. Pick a number from the *Random Number Table*, and add to it any bow skill bonuses to which you are entitled.

If your total score is now 0–6, turn to **245**.
If it is 7 or more, turn to **211**.

108

'Okak nenrak!' growls the Giak, unsheathing his short sword. Your offer of a bribe has aroused his suspicions; he thinks you have stolen the Zlanbeast and he intends to kill you, thereby securing promotion for himself.

Aarnak Giak Sentry:
COMBAT SKILL 17   ENDURANCE 20

If you win the combat, turn to **52**.

109

You are fighting a horde of winged Crypt Spawn. You cannot evade this combat and must fight the loathsome creatures to the death.

Crypt Spawn Flood:
COMBAT SKILL 30   ENDURANCE 36

If you win the combat, turn to **255**.

110 — *Illustration VII*

The deck heaves and shudders, and the metallic whirr of the ironclad's engine rises to a deafening roar as it fights to extricate itself from the stern of the sinking *Intrepid*. Then a war horn blares, signalling to the enemy troops to break off their attack and return to their vessels. Everywhere you look Drakkarim marines and Sommlending crewmen are sheathing their weapons and scrambling towards the ship's rail. Clouds of acrid yellow smoke waft across the decks, adding to the chaos and confusion as scores of men hurl themselves into the dark waves of the Kaltesee.

'Jump!' shouts Davan.

VII.   Scores of men hurl themselves over the ship's rail into the Kaltesee

'But what about the captain?' you reply, anxiously.

'Forget the captain,' he says, pointing at the enemy craft. 'No one can help him now. The ironclad that rammed our stern completely demolished his cabin. No one could have lived through that.'

You pull yourself over the rail and wait for the smoke to thin before you leap. But the *Intrepid* lurches violently, and, before you can stop yourself, you slip and fall head-first into the swirling yellow smog.

Pick a number from the *Random Number Table*.

If the number you have picked is *0–4*, turn to **194**.
If it is *5–9*, turn to **16**.

111

You duck behind a boulder, then immediately begin crawling on your stomach towards another large rock. The slippery shingle aids your progress, but the scrunching sound of enemy footfalls is growing ever louder and you begin to fear that they will catch up with you before you can slip away.

Pick a number from the *Random Number Table*. Add 1 to this number for every Magnakai Discipline you possess in excess of three disciplines (for example, if you possess five disciplines, add 2 to the number you have picked).

If your total is now *0–7*, turn to **8**.
If it is *8* or more, turn to **279**.

112

The creature soon accepts that you are its new master and becomes totally obedient to your commands. It lowers its head and allows you to climb on to its back, where you settle into a comfortable saddle, high-backed and luxuriously padded. A tug on the gem-encrusted reins, and the Zlanbeast takes to the air, climbing with breathtaking speed into the night sky. High above the ironclad fleet, you turn the beast towards the west and begin a journey that you pray will end safely in Aarnak.

Turn to **36**.

113

Davan, and the remnants of his crew, are clinging in desperation to the flotsam that surrounds their dying ship. Many are wounded and their pitiful cries for help can clearly be heard aboard the Drakkarim ironclad. The enemy captain watches them through narrowed eyes, an evil sneer spreading slowly across his brutal face as he reaches for the mechanism that will launch a fire-missile into their midst.

If you have a bow and wish to fire at the captain to prevent him from murdering your fellow countrymen, turn to **131**.

If you do not have a bow, or do not wish to fire at the captain, turn to **239**.

114

You sense the creature weaken as your psychic barrier prevents your fear, that it needs in order to maintain its strength, from escaping. It howls its ghostly frustration and launches itself at your throat.

Mind Reaper: COMBAT SKILL 24   ENDURANCE 32

This supernatural creature is especially susceptible to psychic attack. Double all bonuses you would normally receive if you choose to use either Mindblast or Psi-surge during the combat.

If you win the combat, turn to **306**.

The lookouts are naturally curious about the only passenger aboard their ship, especially as he keeps company with Guildmaster Banedon, the most highly respected magician in Sommerlund. They question you keenly about your mission to Durenor, but when you insist that you are sworn to secrecy, they pursue the matter no further — with you at least.

You learn that they hail from the Kirlundin Isles, a fiefdom famed for its brave and intrepid seafarers, whose ships have protected the coasts of Sommerlund for more than a thousand years. It shocks you deeply to learn that, during your exile in the Daziarn, the Darklords have destroyed the Kirlundin fleet and laid to waste the once fertile isles.

'We'll soon free our isles from that vile cur Gnaag,' growls one disgruntled sailor. The others echo his sentiment, but behind their bravado you sense their fear that they may never live to see their islands free again.

A brooding silence descends on the deck and you decide it would be wise to get some rest before dawn breaks. One of the ship's mates volunteers to show you to your quarters, and you accept his help gratefully.

Turn to **24**.

116

The passage descends for several hundred yards before it levels out and becomes far wider. Beetle-shaped gems embedded in the walls radiate a flickering white glow that bathes this section of the tunnel in a ghostly light, and, as you move along it, you notice a figure in the middle distance, limping towards you. You recognize the figure to be a Liganim, dressed in a silver-grey hooded robe that is identical to the one you wear.

If you wish to try to hide from this creature, turn to **46**.

If you decide to ignore him and continue along the tunnel, turn to **160**.

117

The western face of the Durncrag Mountains is a sheer wall of granite that rises over six thousand feet to a peak known as Mount Lajakodak. To attempt to scale this wall, especially at night and with little equipment, is a formidable and perilous task. For several hours, you search the scree-covered slopes in the hope of finding an old or disused trail, but with no success. You are on the brink of abandoning all hope of finding another route, and are about to return to the Giak outpost, when you chance upon the remains of a track that snakes its way towards an opening high in the rock wall.

If you have the Magnakai Discipline of Huntmastery and have reached the Kai rank of Archmaster, turn to **34**.

If you do not possess this skill, or have yet to reach this level of Kai training, you can either climb the track and investigate the opening: turn to **143**.

Or you can return to the Giak outpost and attempt to scale the wall: turn to **86**.

118

'Kordak Duganok! Jatnar!' squeals the Giak driver, waving his whip frantically in your direction. 'Ok zee dik zek kog lajakim!'

The sharp-eyed Giak has spotted you among the boulders. At once the Drakkarim horsemen respond to his alarm; they spur their mounts to a gallop and come thundering towards you. Before you can attempt to escape, they have surrounded you, dismounted, and are stalking forward with their swords drawn.

If you have a bow and wish to use it, turn to **231**.

If you do not have a bow, or do not wish to use it, turn to **45**.

119

A look of horror washes over the Drakkar's face as he sees you raise your bow and let loose your arrow at his head. Your shaft penetrates his forehead, and the force of the shot lifts him clear of the deck and knocks him flat on his back. Just then the first of his troops appear at the rail. For a moment they hesitate when they see their officer dead, but their shock soon turns to fury. 'Shez dot got!' they scream, and come thundering towards you with murder blazing in their eyes.

If you wish to evade their attack, turn to **274**.
If you choose to stand your ground and receive their attack, turn to **347**.

120

The leading minions reach the end of the alley and turn to the south, following your footprints in the slime. One of them, a Liganim armed with a steel bow, draws an odd-shaped arrow from his quiver and takes aim at your back as you disappear rapidly along the smoky street. You hear the unmistakable hiss of an arrow in flight and instinctively you throw yourself to the ground. As you slide face-first along the filthy street, you feel an agonizing chill as the arrow penetrates your shoulder.

You have been struck by a Zejar-dulaga, a magical arrow impregnated with a deadly poison. You try to stand but your legs feel incapable of supporting your weight and your vision swims in and out of focus.

If you possess the Magnakai Discipline of Curing, and have reached the Kai rank of Mentora or more, turn to **13**.

If you do not possess this skill, or have yet to reach this level of Kai training, turn to **38**.

121

One of the group manages to avoid the rain of deadly blows that slay his companions. He screams with terror, his mind unhinged by the fear of death. Like a wild animal he claws at your chest in his panic to get away and, by chance, he tears the Golden Amulet from the chain around your neck. Before you can stop him, he escapes along the tunnel, clutching it in his bloodstained claws.

If you possess the Magnakai Discipline of Nexus, and have attained the Kai rank of Archmaster, turn to **220**.

If you do not possess this skill, or have yet to reach this level of Kai training, turn to **331**.

122

You try to fend off the speeding arrow, but it passes over your outstretched arm and lodges deep in your skull. For a split second you feel nothing. Then a star-burst of pain rips through your head and a swirl of colour obliterates your vision as you pass swiftly into the timeless oblivion of death.

Your life and your mission end here.

123

Your strength and Kai skill carry you over the gap and back safely to the start of the trail. Quickly you retrace your tracks to the Giak outpost, where you take cover and concentrate on finding a way to get past it.

Turn to **86**.

124

At once you sense that you have stumbled into an area of the city that is the domain of Darklord Taktaal and his followers. You scan the shadows and windows and notice several pairs of watchful eyes regarding you with naked hatred. Slowly you back away from the square, but you have taken less than a dozen steps when a line of creatures begins to emerge from a doorway to your right. They growl menacingly, their feral eyes aglow with blood-lust.

Pick a number from the *Random Number Table*. If you have completed the Lore-circle of Solaris, add 4 to the number you have picked.

If your total is now *0–4*, turn to **342**.
If it is *5* or more, turn to **48**.

125

Slowly, as though awakening from a dream, you return to consciousness. Through half-open eyes you stare at a darkening sky and feel the cold waves of the Kaltesee lapping at your feet. Every inch of your body aches viciously — it is as if your flesh were one vast bruise — but at once you know that your body is intact and that, miraculously, you have escaped serious injury.

126

You are lying in a cup-shaped piece of wreckage that was once part of the ironclad's bow. On the horizon there is now only one ship — the ironclad that first attacked the *Intrepid*. It is silhouetted against the wall of oily flame that marks the place where its sister craft exploded. The tide has carried you away from the carnage, and, turning your head stiffly, you see that the shore lies less than a hundred yards away.

If you possess the Magnakai Discipline of Huntmastery and have reached the rank of Principalin or more, turn to **296**.

If you do not possess this skill, or have yet to reach this level of Kai training, turn to **327**.

126

The sergeant stares at the gold coins and, without raising his head, he shouts a terse order to his troops: 'Jeg tok! Tok narg gaz dik!' Like a herd of angry bulls, the Death Knights rush forward and surround you, their spears held ready to slay you should you show any sign of resisting.

Cursing vilely, the sergeant drags you from the saddle and tears the battle-mask from your face. More guards appear, mostly armed with bows, which they train on you while the sergeant strips you of your weapons and equipment. Then, after tying your hands, they march you to their barracks where you are imprisoned in an empty, steel-walled cell and left alone to contemplate your fate.

Turn to **250**.

127

Using your Kai skill, you magnify your vision and scan the buildings below. You see a maze of garbage-choked streets, rusting tenements, and squalid slave huts. All bear the effects of the corrosive atmosphere, except one building, which is situated near the centre of the city. It is a tower, tall and unbent, its surface free from any sign of decay.

Confident that you have found where the Slavemaster resides, you bring the Zlanbeast in to land nearby. A Giak, his mouth hanging open in awe of your arrival, stands guard at the tower entrance. As you approach, he bows and stands aside, allowing you to enter the gloomy ground floor.

Turn to **346**.

128

You draw the sun-sword from its korlinium scabbard and instantly the blade is caressed by cool, golden flames. The Drakkar leader freezes in his tracks, his eyes bulging fit to burst as he stares with awe at the magical Sommerswerd.

'Naog!' he breathes, incredulously. 'Gadajok-shezag! Aki-amaz! Okak naog gaj!' He hesitates, then begins to retreat towards the rail. At this moment the first of his troops clamber on to the deck. Fearful of the consequences should he be branded a coward in their eyes, he shouts a battle-cry and commands them to attack.

'Shez dot got!' they scream, and come thundering towards you with murder blazing in their cruel, inhuman eyes.

If you wish to evade their attack, turn to **274**.
If you decide to stand your ground and receive their attack, turn to **39**.

129 — *Illustration VIII*

Guided by your instructions, Captain Borse commands his helmsman to steer 'hard a' port', a manoeuvre that will take the *Intrepid* clear of the enemy line. Swiftly the ship changes course. You watch the Darkland ironclads looming larger with each passing minute, and note the formidable array of weapons aboard their steel-skinned decks. Huge, black funnels protrude from the middle of each craft, which emit clouds of choking, sulphurous smoke. As the *Intrepid* rounds the last ironclad in the line, this acrid smoke wafts across the water and engulfs the crew, causing them to cough and retch violently. The sound of their coughing alerts the enemy lookouts who immediately raise the alarm.

Suddenly, a flash of blue-white light illuminates the bow of the ironclad and a fiery projectile arcs across the sky towards the *Intrepid*.

Pick a number from the *Random Number Table*.

If the number you have picked is *0–6*, turn to **20**.
If it is *7–9*, turn to **180**.

130

You follow the passage for nearly an hour before you happen upon something that raises your flagging

VIII.   The Darkland ironclads surge towards the *Intrepid*

spirits. At a junction with two other tunnels your eye is drawn to a large emblem that has been chiselled skilfully out of the granite wall. It is a depiction of a snake's skull with two fly-like eyes, surrounded by a circle of fire. At once you recognize this carving: it is the personal emblem of Darklord Gnaag. You study the sign: it must mark the start of a tunnel that leads to the Imperial Sector of the city.

With your pulse racing, you set off along the torchlit tunnel. You have not gone very far when you see that it ends at a large steel door, guarded by two monstrous creatures clad in heavy plate mail. A smaller door appears to your left, and, as you draw level with it, you reach out and turn its handle. The door is locked.

If you possess a Black Key, turn to **278**.
If you do not possess this Backpack Item, turn to **29**.

131

The captain arches his back and screams in agony as your arrow drives deep into his spine. Immediately, two Drakkarim gunners rush forward to help him, but as soon as they realize that he is dead, they spin around to confront you.

If you have at least two arrows and wish to silence these Drakkarim, turn to **259**.
If you choose to draw a hand weapon and attack them before they can alert their shipmates, turn to **292**.

132

Holding your breath, you unsheathe your weapon and press yourself to the cliff wall. You plan to take the approaching Giaks by surprise, cut your way through them to the summit, then escape before the pursuing group can catch up. It is a bold manoeuvre and one that does not allow for the night-sharp eyes and cruel cunning of the Giak commander. From his position atop the cliff he watches your every move.

'Koga!' he shouts, and both search parties freeze in their tracks. 'Dulaga zaj!' Suddenly there is a sound like rushing water, then a terrible pain rips through your chest as you are hit by a score of black arrows, fired by Giak archers kneeling at the edge of the cliff. You gasp for breath as a terrifying numbness spreads throughout your body. Although you fight to stay on your feet, you can no longer feel your legs. Stiffly you fall from the path and crash to your doom on the beach below.

Your life and your mission end here on the shores of the Darklands.

133

Your hand closes around the hilt of the black sword moments before Kraagenskûl's claw-tipped fingers rake the floor where it lay. You raise the blade and feel a surge of cold power run the length of your arm. It courses through your brain, willing you to attack the cowering Darklord and slaughter him unmercifully. This new-felt need to wallow in the killing of an enemy stirs you to a fearful rage. Desperately you draw on your inner strength to overcome this barbaric urge, and control it, as you prepare to fight with Darklord Kraagenskûl.

Darklord Kraagenskûl (without Helshezag):
COMBAT SKILL 35   ENDURANCE 38

This supernatural being is immune to Mindblast (but not Psi-surge). Owing to the power of Helshezag — the weapon you now wield — add 7 to your COMBAT SKILL for the duration of the combat.

If you win the combat, turn to **240**.

134

Once more the pit is cleared and the spectators settle down to enjoy another round of vicious hand-to-hand fighting. The next two combatants are poised to enter the ring and, in the light of what happened previously, they have both decided to ignore the gong and tear into each other as soon as their holding cage door slides open.

Bets are about to be placed when the sound of a loud, intermittent whistle interrupts the proceedings: it is the signal that Helgedad has been sighted by the lookout. Some of the crowd leave their seats in order to view the Black City through the tiny portholes that line the walls of the gallery. With your heart pounding at the thought of seeing the Darkland's most infamous stronghold for the first time, you leave the pit and join them.

Turn to **326**.

135

As you fight to stay on your feet, the beast bears down, tilting its head from side to side, revealing just a glimpse of your target. Guided by instinct alone you raise your bow and fire.

Pick a number from the *Random Number Table*, and add to this number any bow skill bonuses to which you are entitled.

If your total is now *0–8*, turn to **313**.
If it is 9 or more, turn to **105**.

136

You draw on your Kai skill to neutralize the deadly venom that is coursing through your veins. Swiftly your powers of healing overcome the poison, but at a cost of 4 ENDURANCE points. You prise the hideous creature off your head and hurl it to the floor, but no sooner has it hit the steel deck than it springs back at your face, forcing you to defend yourself.

Plaak: COMBAT SKILL 30   ENDURANCE 10

This creature is immune to Mindblast and Psi-surge. Owing to the speed and shock of its attack, unless you possess the Magnakai Discipline of Huntmastery, you are unable to draw a weapon and must fight the first round of combat unarmed.

If you win the combat, turn to **218**.

137

Guided by starlight, you trek westwards through the pass until the need for food and rest forces you to stop. A brief search uncovers a shallow fissure in the mountain wall which offers a safe refuge for the night, and there you decide to grab a few hours' sleep before continuing to Argazad. You must now eat a Meal or lose 3 ENDURANCE points.

Turn to **165**.

The crystal shard emits a tinkling, bell-like sound, and the guard moves aside to allow you to enter the Tower of the Damned. He points to a column of bright blue light, descending from the darkness above, and tells you to step into its shimmering rays. You hesitate, and he laughs mockingly at your indecision.

'Go on, step in. It's quicker than climbing the stairs.' Your Kai senses tell you that the column is a beam of partial gravity, a transportation device that will draw you slowly towards the top of the tower.

You step into the light and feel youself rising. Minutes later, the sensation stops and you step from the beam into a huge, domed chamber. The polished walls and floor glisten like the mirrored surfaces of a black lake. The aura of evil hangs everywhere like a thick mist. It closes your throat and threatens to suffocate you. Your heart pounds loudly as you move towards a dais at the centre of the chamber, where a machine rests that matches the description of the Transfusor that Lord Rimoah gave you before leaving Toran. You reach for your backpack, but before you can lift your robe and unshoulder it, the chamber is filled with a roaring growl.

'What brings you here, vermin of Ghanesh?'

It is the voice of Darklord Taktaal. From the shadows of an archway, he slithers towards the dais, his smooth, ice-white head swaying upon a fur-covered snake body, riddled with disease. Your stomach turns as you watch a muzzle distend from his face, then split open to reveal a row of razor-sharp fangs. Seemingly you are a lowly follower of his hated rival, Darklord

Ghanesh, and you know that if you are to survive you must answer his command convincingly.

> If you wish to tell him that you want to defect from Ghanesh's service, and serve him instead, turn to **261**.
>
> If you wish to tell him that you have secret information that could destroy Ghanesh, turn to **168**.

139

The Death Knight sentinel stiffens and falls dead at your feet, his black armour and his black heart torn open by the force of your killing blow. A quick search of his body reveals the following items:

> SPEAR
> DAGGER
> AXE
> POUCH OF TOBACCO
> BOTTLE OF WINE
> PIPE
> 60 KIKA (equivalent to 6 Gold Crowns)
> IRON KEY
> ENOUGH FOOD FOR 1 MEAL

If you wish to keep any of the above items, make the necessary adjustments to your *Action Chart*.

To continue, turn to **257**.

140

Beyond the door lies a corridor that leads to a narrow hall of stone. Its ceiling, flat and undomed, is supported by thick columns that march in rows down the sides of the walls. Between the columns are plain steel doors, the largest one guarded by Death Knights. From the safety of the shadows you watch as this great door swings open and a man, swathed in a voluminous scarlet robe, emerges into the corridor. He speaks at length with the two guards, who depart in haste when he has finished, as if running an important errand. Beyond the great door you can see a flight of stairs ascending into darkness. The man in red watches the Death Knights leave, then turns and ascends the stairs hurriedly, leaving the great steel door ajar.

Hoping that this staircase leads to the roof, you cross the corridor and follow the robed man, taking care not to be seen, as you stalk silently in his wake. Your Kai skills keep you hidden from view and enable you to gain entry to the chamber that occupies the entire top floor of this building. There you take cover behind one of many statues that encircle the floor, and witness a scene that chills you to the core.

Turn to **216**.

141

Your mastery of mental power enables you to shield your mind from the psychic probe emanating from the box-like device that the guard is using to check your identity. Because of your effective mindshield, he is unable to detect any hostile psychic signals. Satisfied that it is safe to allow you to pass, he orders his fellow guard to open the steel door and let you into the subterranean levels of the Imperial Sector.

Beyond the door is a vast hall filled with row upon row of fearsome weapons. It is the Imperial Armoury of Helgedad.

If you possess a Black Cube, turn to **40**.
If you do not possess this item, turn to **320**.

142

'What have we here?' muses the captain warily, as he accepts your envelope. 'Guildmaster Banedon instructed me to deliver this into your charge as soon as we cleared the blockade,' you reply. 'It contains confidential details about our voyage to Durenor.'

'I'm sure the matter can wait 'til morning,' he says slipping the envelope into the pocket of his gold braided jacket. 'You'd best get some sleep. We could be in for some rough weather come sunrise.' You insist that he read the contents of the letter without delay but he dismisses your request with a flick of his calloused hand. 'It can wait. A few hours'll make no odds,' he snaps, and he descends the stairs before you can argue otherwise.

If you wish to accompany the first mate to your cabin, turn to **24**.

(continued over)

If you decide to stay on the forecastle with the lookouts, turn to **115**.

143

In daylight, the trail is steep and treacherous, but in the cold, starlit darkness it is doubly so. Chunks of rock crumble underfoot and in many places there is simply no trail at all. Progress can only be made by inching yourself painfully across the sheer drops, using your fingers and what little of the ledge that remains. Eventually you reach the dark opening and enter with trepidation. A smooth, semi-circular tunnel descends through the rock. The passage is lit faintly by an eerie ochre light, which is cast by clumps of bacteria that seem to thrive on the damp tunnel walls.

If you possess the Magnakai Discipline of Curing, turn to **93**.

If you do not possess this skill, turn to **303**.

144

There is another knock, this time more insistent, but when you do not open the door your uninvited visitor does not knock again. Tired and hungry, you must now eat a Meal or lose 3 ENDURANCE points before you settle down to sleep. You awake to the sound of a loud click, barely audible above the ever-present din of the Lajakeka's engine: your cabin door has just closed. Swiftly you rise and rush to the door, hoping to catch a glimpse of whoever, or whatever, gained access to your cabin while you slept.

If you possess the Magnakai Discipline of Animal Control, and have reached the Kai rank of Mentora or more, turn to **273**.

If you do not possess this skill, or have yet to reach this level of Kai training, turn to **98**.

145

At once you recognize the pungent aroma of Adgana leaves. Adgana is a powerful narcotic that increases strength and sharpens reflexes; it enhances fighting prowess when swallowed immediately prior to combat. There is sufficient Adgana in this pouch for one dose, which would be enough to increase your COMBAT SKILL by 6 points for the duration of a fight.

But be warned! Adgana is shunned by most warriors and its use is outlawed in Sommerlund because it is highly addictive. If you choose to keep and use this Dose of Adgana prior to combat, there is a chance that *you* could become addicted. As soon as combat is resolved, you must pick a number from the *Random Number Table*. If the number you pick is 0 or 1, you have become addicted and your ENDURANCE score must be reduced by 4 points immediately. If you have ever used Adgana in a previous Lone Wolf adventure, the risks of addiction are doubled should you decide to use this dose (you will become addicted if you pick a 0, 1, 2, or 3 on the *Random Number Table*). Also, the effects of the narcotic when used on a second or subsequent occasion are halved. You will be able to add only 3 points to your COMBAT SKILL, instead of 6). If you decide to keep this Dose of Adgana, note the hazardous side effects of its use in the margin of your *Action Chart*.

Sure that you have not overlooked any other items that could aid your perilous mission, you decide the time has come to leave.

Turn to **274**.

146

Shortly after dawn has brightened the eastern horizon, the Drakkar warrior appears, riding his steed unhurriedly along the trail to Argazad. As he approaches, you get ready to launch your ambush.

If you have a bow and wish to use it, turn to **99**.

If you do not have a bow, or do not wish to use one, you must leap on the Drakkar as soon as he rides within range: turn to **64**.

147

The two Vassagonians unsheathe their rapier-thin swords and advance towards you, secretly thankful that they are no longer the target of Kraagenskûl's wrath. The Darklord orders them to halt and demands that you step within the circle of the fiery pillars and explain your intrusion. You sense that he has not detected your true identity, that his psychic skills are solely destructive, and that he is, for now, deceived by your Drakkarim disguise.

'I have come from the victorious army of Darklord Xog, the conqueror of Cloeasia, with vital information to impart, O Mighty Lord of Darkness,' you say, slavishly. You speak partly in Vassagonian and partly in Giak to maintain your deception. 'There is a traitor in your court. He has tried to send word to the enemy, to warn them of what is being constructed in Argazad. I know who he is and I carry proof of his treachery.'

'Speak!' commands Kraagenskûl. 'Speak or die!'

'I shall speak, O Invincible Lord of Death and Decay, but I crave your confidence. Can we not speak alone?' You cast an accusing glance at the two Vassagonians, and they return your look with fear and hatred blazing in their eyes.

'Leave us!' snarls Kraagenskûl, pointing to the stairs with his jet-black blade, 'but stray no further than the hall below, and do not disturb us until I call for you.'

Reluctantly, the Vassagonians leave, their heads bowed in reverence but their eyes still fixed murderously on you.

Turn to **286**.

148

The Drakkar officer staggers and falls, clutching his wounds and cursing you with his dying breath. But no sooner has his body hit the planks than his troops come rushing towards you from all sides. 'Sez dot got!' they scream, howling with primal fury, their teeth bared and their faces contorted with rage.

Drakkarim Marines:
COMBAT SKILL 29   ENDURANCE 40

If you win the combat, turn to **28**.

149

As you land on the Drakkar, you grab him in a head lock and drag him from the saddle. The force of your attack twists his neck awry and you hear a sharp crack a moment before you both strike the ground. Quickly you recover from the fall, draw a weapon, and jump on the prone warrior before he can get to his feet. But you soon discover that he is no longer a threat: your attack broke his neck and he was dead before his body hit the ground.

Turn to **79**.

150

A thousand feet below, at the heart of the chasm, a seething carpet of nightmare shapes crawl and slither amid rivers of molten rock. They appear to your horrified eyes to be writhing in perpetual agony, and your psychic senses confirm that this is the case: it is their pain, not their bodies, that feed this raging sea of supernatural flame.

The gates of the Black City open and the Lajakeka passes into this terrible realm of evil, along a vast avenue of steel, flanked by buildings of hellish grandeur and purpose. You can see red flames glaring at peaked gothic windows, and innumerable barred gates that appear like the grinning jaws of dragons. At length, the vehicle grinds to a halt at a place where a huge chute burrows deep into the ground. The crew make preparations to unload their cargo directly into this funnel-shaped hole whilst you and the other passengers disembark. With fear running ice-cold in your veins, you scan the fireswept street and notice that all the other passengers are scurrying towards a tunnel.

If you wish to follow them and enter the tunnel, turn to **80**.

If you choose to avoid them and the tunnel, and prefer to explore the street, turn to **197**.

151

The *Intrepid* responds to the wheel, and, as the wind fills out her sails, she begins to pull away from the first ironclad. Your hopes rise but they are soon dashed when a jolt runs through the deck and she rolls back towards the enemy vessel. Then you see why you cannot escape.

'Davan! Quick, have your men cut the grappling lines!' you shout. Immediately he urges his men to carry out your command. Anxiously you watch as the second ironclad bears down on the stern with unnerving speed. The lines are soon severed and you feel the ship swing about, yet the enemy craft is almost upon you, its deck crammed with more troops, poised to leap aboard. Suddenly it hits the rear quarter, and you are knocked down by the shock. The screech of tortured metal and the crack of splintering wood fill the air, yet the deck soon rights itself and you are able to regain control of the helm. Despite the shock of impact and the fearful noise, the enemy craft has only glanced the bow, its steel-tipped ram missing the rudder by just a few feet. It scrapes alongside before veering away amid a cloud of foul, yellow smoke.

The crew cheer and the Drakkarim marines falter as they watch their vessels slipping away to the stern. The battle on board turns in your favour, and, as Davan and his men press their advantage, you feel sure that the *Intrepid* will make a successful escape along the coast.

Within the space of a few minutes your confidence is shattered anew by an unexpected attack.

Turn to **74**.

152

The swiftness of your reactions, and the degree of psychic mastery you have attained, save you from sustaining any injury to your central nervous system. Rapidly the shock fades, leaving you alert and ready to face Darklord Kraagenskûl.

Turn to **147**.

153

The creature thrashes the last of its death-throes, then falls silent, its great bulk all but filling the entrance to the cave. The stench of spilt blood, and the greasy, dirt-encrusted hair that covers its torso, makes your stomach churn. Yet the Egorgh's body is serving a useful purpose. Not only is it keeping the icy cold wind and rain at bay, but any other creature wanting to attack you would have great difficulty entering the cave. Confident that you are unlikely to be disturbed again, you settle down to a much-needed sleep.

Turn to **300**.

154

You follow the Slavemaster into a chamber filled with marvellous treasures, furniture, and rich trappings, which seem anachronistic here in this foul city. He advises you to take off your Drakkar armour and wear instead a hooded robe woven from a strange, silver-grey material. He comments favourably on the Golden Amulet you wear, assuring you that its protection will be essential for your survival in Helgedad. As you are about to don the robe, he insists that you wear your backpack underneath it. 'The creature who donated this garment, albeit it reluctantly, was tall but possessed a severely crooked spine. In order to gain entry to Helgedad you must pretend to be that creature. The pack will help to complete your disguise.'

You ask the identity of the creature, and what has become of him. 'He was one of the Liganim, those who assist the Nadziranim sorcerers with their black arts,' replies the Slavemaster. 'This particular Liganim came here to Aarnak to fetch a quantity of special grade ore for his master's experiments, but the unfortunate creature met with a fatal accident, here in this very chamber.' The trace of a smile on the Slavemaster's face suggests that the accident may not have been quite so accidental.

'How am I to get into Helgedad?' you ask, hoping he has planned for this as well.

'You will be told in good time, but first I must give you some other information that is vital to the success of your quest.'

Turn to **235**.

155

The sound of heavy footfalls and vile curses alert you to a group of marines who are charging along the deck, drawn by their comrade's dying scream. They see him fall dead at your feet and, in a rage, the leading warrior hurls his sword at your head.

Pick a number from the *Random Number Table*. If you have the Magnakai Discipline of Huntmastery, add 1 to the number you have picked. If you have completed the Lore-circle of Solaris, add 3 to the number.

If your total is now *0–2*, turn to **341**.
If it is *3–8*, turn to **9**.
If it is *9* or more, turn to **319**.

156

The screams of your pursuers are growing louder with every passing second. Fearful that they will alert the guard to your presence, you unsheathe a hand weapon and stalk forward, grimly determined to slay the robed creature as quickly and quietly as possible.

If you have completed the Lore-circle of Solaris, turn to **190**.
If you have not completed this Lore-circle of the Magnakai, turn to **56**.

157

After following the coastline northwards for an hour, you happen upon a narrow path that rises from the beach and zig-zags up to the top of the cliffs. The path appears deserted, and you decide to use it rather than risk being caught by the rising tide.

The climb to the top is long and arduous and by the time you reach the peak, the weather has taken a turn for the worse. An icy, rain-laden wind whips inland from the sea, its chilling bite accompanied by sheet lightning that illuminates the stark landscape before you. The blue-white flash reveals a vast, dead world of pitted spurs and crags, where every tree is petrified and every rock looks like a dead man's skull. You pull your warm cape close about your shoulders and set off towards a ridge that is peppered with dark hollows. You pray that one of them will offer some shelter from the coming storm.

Upon reaching the ridge, you discover that most of the hollows are merely patches of dark earth sandwiched between the honeycombed rock. The rain has become torrential, and you are about to abandon all hope of finding dry shelter, when suddenly your tracking instincts alert you to a cave-like opening at the far end of the ridge. You investigate and discover that it is indeed the entrance to a cave, one that is both wind- and watertight and, to your relief, quite empty. You are now very hungry and must eat a Meal or lose 3 ENDURANCE points.

If you have the Magnakai Discipline of Animal Control *and* Divination, turn to **234**.

If you do not possess *both* these skills, turn to **307**.

158 — *Illustration IX (overleaf)*

Alerted by the Zlanbeast's wild screech, the Death Knight spins around and catches your blow on the haft of his spear. Sparks and curses fly. Growling like an angry lion, he pushes you away then stabs viciously at your midriff. Ice-cool nerve and fleetness of foot

IX. The Death Knight stabs viciously at your midriff

save you from the razor-sharp tip, and quickly you return the strike, forcing the Drakkar back to the edge of the parapet with the speed and determination of your attack.

Death Knight Sentinel:
COMBAT SKILL 28   ENDURANCE 29

If you win the fight, turn to **139**.

159

Shock, as a result of his severe leg injuries, has reduced the captain's blood pressure to a dangerously low level. Your mastery of the discipline of Curing enables you to increase his blood pressure gently to ensure that his brain is not starved of its vital supply of oxygen. Once he is stable, the first mate, whose name is Davan, helps you splint the captain's legs and construct a makeshift stretcher on which to carry him to his cabin. Slowly he regains consciousness, and, although he is in great pain, he insists on speaking.

'Davan,' he says, through gritted teeth, 'the ship's under your command now. You must do all you can to see that our passenger reaches his destination.' Dutifully, the first mate promises to obey the captain's order. 'Open the chest,' the captain says, motioning with his eyes to a large casket, resting at the foot of his bunk. You oblige and discover that it contains a vest made of finely crafted bronin chainmail, and a pair of engraved silver bracers designed to protect the forearms during combat. 'Take them, friend,' he says, 'they may be of some help to you on your journey.'

The Bronin Vest adds 3 points to your COMBAT SKILL and 1 to your ENDURANCE. The Silver Bracers add

2 points to your COMBAT SKILL and 1 to your ENDURANCE. If you wish to keep either (or both) the Bronin Vest or the Silver Bracers, mark them on your *Action Chart* as Special Items, which you wear accordingly.

Turn to **262**.

160

At your approach, the Liganim slows and makes a sign in the air with his warty hand. When you fail to respond, he becomes agitated and moves directly in front of you to block your way. A tingling sensation ripples your scalp as a wave of psychic energy washes over your mind. The Liganim has probed your thoughts and discovered that you are an imposter. He emits a high-pitched shriek and unsheathes a dagger from his belt as he launches himself maniacally at your chest.

Liganim: COMBAT SKILL 25   ENDURANCE 26

Unless you possess the Magnakai Discipline of Psi-screen, deduct 1 ENDÚRANCE point at the beginning of every round of combat, owing to the Liganim's persistent psychic attacks.

If you win the combat, turn to **246**.

161

Shaking your head, you pull yourself to your feet and force your eyes to focus on the swirling shapes that are looming out of the shadows. Four ugly Giaks are creeping towards you, each with a loaded bow held ready to fire. They let loose their arrows and instantly you throw yourself back on to the ground. Your reactions save you from the deadly shafts, and you scramble quickly to your feet, unsheathing a weapon. You catch the enemy wrong-footed and without their swords to hand.

Giak Archers: COMBAT SKILL 14   ENDURANCE 22

If you win the combat, turn to **349**.

162

The Zlanbeast glides through the rising steam and lands smoothly beside the foundry's rusty wall. The air, or what passes for air in this doom-laden city, reeks of iron and soot, and, as you jump from the saddle, you discover that the ground is covered with a layer of soot several inches deep.

On a ramp that services the foundry, a line of stunted, lizard-like bipeds are hauling heavy carts full of ore. They are watched by Giaks who encourage them with kicks and curses whenever they falter. A Giak officer and two of his troops leave the ramp as soon as they see you land and come scurrying towards you. The officer is shouting at the top of his voice. You sense that he suspects you have stolen the Zlanbeast and is demanding that you explain, on pain of death!

If you wish to ignore his threats and demand that he take you to the Slavemaster, turn to **27**.

If you have any Kika, and wish to offer them to the Giak as a bribe for safe escort to the Slavemaster, turn to **43**.

163

Your senses alert you to the magical chainmail armour that the Drakkar warrior is wearing beneath his leather battle-jacket. He can see that you are aiming your arrow at his heart and he is confident that his armour will protect him.

> If you wish to switch targets and aim instead at his head, turn to **119**.

> If you choose to shoulder your bow and meet his attack with a hand weapon, turn to **213**.

164

No sooner has the last of your enemies fallen than you sense that more of them are about to emerge from the surrounding towers. There is no time to search the bodies of the slain — to stay would be suicidal. Without hesitation, you turn on your heel and run for all you are worth.

Turn to **48**.

165

Shortly after dawn, a howling wind awakens you from your dreamless slumber. It sweeps along the pass from the west, carrying with it the briny smell of the sea. Resolutely you continue your trek, following the roadway through the pass until, at midday, you emerge from the mountains at a point that commands a clear view over the land beyond. There you stop and stare at an expanse of rocky terrain so fragmented that it might have been smashed by a giant hammer. It slopes down to the shores of a wide inlet – the Gulf of Helenag – where a line of Darkland ironclads are steaming northwards on their way to join the blockade. From where you are, they appear no larger than tiny black specks dotting the steel-grey sea, but the clouds of yellow smoke that pour from their funnels clearly identify them as enemy ships.

The track continues, snaking southwards across the barren landscape on its way to Argazad. For three hours you tread its uneven surface until you arrive at what appears to be the ruins of an ancient tower.

If you possess the Magnakai Discipline of Divination and have attained the Kai rank of Mentora or higher, turn to **323**.

If you do not possess this skill, or have yet to reach this level of Kai training, turn to **191**.

166

'Three months ago, on the day that you Sommlending celebrate your Feast of Fehmarn, I foresaw in a dream your return to this world, the place and the hour of your coming,' says Rimoah, reverently. 'I, and all my brothers, held this dream to be a sign from the god Kai that you had not died at Torgar, and since that day we have prepared for your return so that we may help you fulfil your vow and deliver us all from the tyranny of the Darklords. With the aid of Guildmaster Banedon we have conceived a plan that can secure a lasting victory. Defeat of the Darklords on the field of battle is now impossible; the allied armies are greatly outnumbered and are hard pressed to protect what little remains of the freelands. The only way in which we can rid ourselves of this evil is by destroying Gnaag and the Transfusor – the device that transmits power to the Tanoz-tukor. Both of them are in Helgedad.'

To hear the name of that foul city spoken aloud is enough to send a shiver down your spine, and the thought of daring to venture there to destroy its ruler fills you with cold dread. 'It is a daunting task that we ask you to attempt, Lone Wolf,' says Banedon, sensing your anxiety, 'but only you have any hope of succeeding in this desperate mission. It may be of some comfort to learn that, with the Darklords leading their armies in the field, the defences of the Black City are now at their weakest. Only Gnaag and his second-in-command, Darklord Taktaal, reside there at present.'

'You spoke of a plan?' you say, returning your gaze to the wise face of Lord Rimoah. Without replying, he bends down and pulls out a leather sack from beneath the chair on which he sat when you entered the chamber. It contains what appears to be a mass of triangular crystals that are fused together. At once you recognize its purpose. It is a powerful charge, similar to the one which Lord Adamas used to destroy the Torgar Gate.

'This will put paid to the Transfusor,' says Rimoah, holding up the crystal explosive. He points to a shard that is longer than the others and informs you that the device is activated by withdrawing and re-inserting it tip-first into the core. 'It must be placed beneath the Transfusor and it will detonate exactly fifteen minutes after it is primed.' Carefully he replaces the explosive into the sack and offers it to you.

'But how am I to gain entry to Helgedad?' you ask, as you accept the deadly package tentatively.

'We have made preparations,' answers Banedon, pointing once more to the map. 'A caravel is anchored in Toran harbour. Under cover of darkness it will run the blockade, then head east to deceive the enemy into thinking that it is bound for Durenor. When safe to do so it will turn about and steer a course for

Dejkaata. The shallows there are free of pack-ice at this time of the year and the captain should be able to land you on the coast close to the Aarnak Estuary. From there you must make your way on foot to the stronghold of Aarnak and seek out the Slavemaster. He is one of our agents and can be trusted. Make yourself known to him by saying the words, "Sommerlund is burning". He alone knows where in Helgedad the Transfusor is located, and he can arrange for your safe and secret passage into the city. Once inside, you must destroy Gnaag and the Transfusor as quickly as possible.'

'And once the task is complete, how then do I effect an escape?' you ask.

'You must make your way back to Aarnak. The demise of the Darklords will announce the success of your mission and we shall then mount an expedition to bring you safely home. But until then, no one must know your true identity, or the reason for your journey to Helgedad.'

Silently you contemplate the awesomeness of this mission, its dangers, and the terrible consequences that will befall Magnamund should you fail. At length you raise your eyes from the map and force a smile. 'When must I leave?' you ask, bravely.

'Tomorrow night,' Banedon replies. 'An hour after sunset.'

Mark the Crystal Explosive on your *Action Chart* as a Special Item that you carry strapped to your Backpack. If you already carry the maximum number of Special Items, you must discard one in favour of the Crystal Explosive.

If you possess the Sommerswerd, turn to **282**.
If you do not possess this Special Item, turn to **229**.

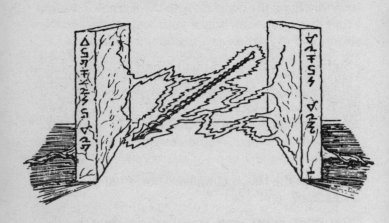

167

The Death Knight sergeant strides forward and repeats his command. When you fail to answer, he reaches up, grabs the front of your leather battle-jacket, and pulls you to within inches of his sneering face. 'Egor sheg!' he growls, and tilts your mask back with the palm of his gloved hand. Using your advanced Kai skill, you cause your face to take on the coarse features of a Drakkarim warrior. The sergeant nods, a look of recognition softening his cruel eyes, then releases his grip of your jacket.

'Agna tok!' he says, turning to face his guards. 'Dok lug shad.' They stand aside and quickly you ride through the gate. A shadowy street lies beyond, at the end of which is a sign that indicates the way to the two main areas of the base: the ironclad harbour and the supply depot.

If you wish to investigate the harbour, turn to **295**.
If you wish to investigate the supply depot, turn to **328**.

168

Suddenly, without warning, the Darklord emits a hideous screech that fills your head with a terrible stabbing pain. Your mind is under attack from a powerful wave of psychic energy that is capable of destroying your free will.

If you possess the Magnakai Discipline of Psi-screen, and have reached the Kai rank of Scion-kai or more, turn to **329**.
If you do not possess this skill, or have yet to reach this level of Kai training, turn to **258**.

169

Stealthily you move away from the door, raising the hood of your cape to hide your face. Beyond the wheelhouse you see a large tube of steel, mounted horizontally on a circular platform. It is attended by three Drakkarim, who are busily loading a heavy, pear-shaped projectile into a chamber at the rear of the tube. A large, wooden crate, filled with several more projectiles, lies open at their feet. Their captain, his rank denoted by the silver braid that decorates the sleeves of his battle-jacket, is pointing to the sinking *Intrepid* and shouting excitedly: 'Gaz muzar ok ruzzar! Shadaegina gag!'

If you possess the Magnakai Disciplines of Invisibility and Pathmanship, turn to **219**.
If you do not possess *both* these skills, turn to **84**.

170 – *Illustration X*

The tunnel grows darker and dirtier the further down it you venture. You are beginning to suspect that you have entered'an abandoned passage when the unmistakable stench of decaying meat wafts past you on a sulphurous breeze. Then two misshapen creatures loom out of the darkness, and your stomach churns at the sight of their hideously swollen faces. Their eyes are slits, the lids sewn down against the putrid flesh of their cheeks by lengths of coarse, black thread. They stagger towards you, their hooked claws scrabbling the air and their long, snake-like tongues flickering from their lipless mouths as hungrily they savour the scent of your flesh.

Helgedad Ghouls:
COMBAT SKILL 23   ENDURANCE 32

These creatures are immune to Mindblast and Psi-surge.

If you possess the Sommerswerd, and wish to use it, turn to **208**.

If you win the combat, turn to **280**.

171

The moment you draw the dagger from your belt, a blue flame courses the length of its twisted blade and the squealing flood of Crypt Spawn soar upward towards the roof in order to avoid you. They and their creator, Darklord Kraagenskûl, recognize the power you wield and both are in awe and terror of it. Freed from the threat of his loathsome summonations, you now advance upon Kraagenskûl with the dagger

X. Two misshapen Helgedad Ghouls loom out of the darkness

before you. He screams in anger and lunges at your head, his sword ablaze with tongues of black fire. You catch the blow on the tip of the dagger and both blades spark furiously as their terrible powers collide.

Darklord Kraagenskûl:
COMBAT SKILL 45   ENDURANCE 48

This supernatural being is immune to Mindblast (but not Psi-surge). You may add 7 points to your COMBAT SKILL for the duration of the fight, owing to the power of the Dagger of Vashna when used against a Darklord of Helgedad.

If you win the combat, turn to **240**.

172

Suddenly, with an ear-splitting crack, the timbers of the main deck collapse and you feel yourself falling headlong into the bowels of the ship. The bulkheads, severely weakened during the Xargath's attack, have finally given way beneath the weight of fighting men and dropped you all into the cargo hold below.

Pick a number from the *Random Number Table* (0 equals 10). If you have completed the Lore-circle of Solaris, deduct 2 from the number you have picked. The final number represents the number of ENDURANCE points you have lost due to injuries sustained in the fall. Make the necessary adjustment to your *Action Chart*.

Turn to **222**.

173

Your Kai skill enables you to escape without leaving any tracks upon the slime-covered streets for your pursuers to follow. When they reach the junction, they cannot be sure in which direction you ran. The minutes lost in indecision give you time to escape from their clutches.

Turn to **48**.

174

Night has fallen swiftly, but there is a full moon by which to see. It pierces the darkness and bathes the landscape in its ghostly, ashen light. The tide bears you swiftly towards a shingle beach that is littered with huge, sea-smoothed boulders. The crashing surf and the screech of predatory seabirds echo all along this barren coastline. It is an unwelcoming sound, cold and hostile, a fitting reflection of the land itself.

Ten yards from the stony beach, you slip into the thigh-deep foam and wade ashore. Although you can see no sign of enemy patrols, you keep your head low as you scurry up the beach towards the base of a sheer cliff wall. By chance you happen upon a narrow path that clings precariously to the side of the cliff-face as it zig-zags its way to the top. The climb is long and arduous, and by the time you reach the summit the weather has taken a turn for the worse. An icy, rain-laden wind whips inland from the sea. Its chilling bite is accompanied by sheet lightning that illuminates the landscape before you. The blue-white flashes reveal a vast, dead world of pitted spurs and crags, where every tree is petrified and every rock looks like a dead man's skull. You pull your cape close about your shoulders and set off towards a ridge that is peppered with dark hollows, hoping that one of them will offer some shelter from the coming storm.

Upon reaching the ridge, you discover that most of the hollows are merely patches of dark earth sandwiched between the honeycombed rock. The rain has become torrential, and you are beginning to abandon all hope of finding dry shelter, when suddenly your tracking instincts alert you to a cave-like opening at the far end of the ridge. You investigate and discover that it is indeed the entrance to a cave, one that is both wind and watertight and, to your relief, quite empty. You are now very hungry and must eat a Meal or lose 3 ENDURANCE points.

If you have the Magnakai Disciplines of Animal Control *and* Divination, turn to **234**.

If you do not possess *both* these skills, turn to **307**.

175

With unexpected speed, the Drakkar jumps to his feet and draws his saw-edged sword. He spits the dust from his mouth and growls a curse as he makes ready to strike a blow at your head.

Drakkar: COMBAT SKILL 19   ENDURANCE 26

If you win the combat, turn to **79**.

176

You know that if you are to destroy this powerful enemy, you must strike quickly and effectively, before he has a chance to retaliate.

If you have the Sommerswerd, and wish to unsheathe it, turn to **208**.

If you possess either the Dagger of Vashna *or* the sword, Helshezag, and wish to use either of them, turn to **230**.

If you have a bow and a Zejar-deluga arrow, and wish to use them, turn to **238**.

If you have none of the above Special Items (or choose not to use them), you can draw a hand weapon: turn to **340**.

177

Using your Magnakai skill, you cause the flames to flicker and die before you sustain any serious burns. Your advanced discipline also protects you from the smoke and fumes given off by the smouldering canvas, and enables you to crawl from under the fallen sails uninjured.

Turn to **181**.

178

Like a shadow, you glide towards the Death Knight, your weapon poised to strike him down, but, just as you are closing for the kill, the Zlanbeast lets out a piercing caw of alarm.

Pick a number from the *Random Number Table*. If you have completed the Lore-circle of Fire *and* the Lore-circle of Solaris, add 1 to this number. If you have the Magnakai Discipline of Animal Control, and have reached the Kai rank of Archmaster, add 3 to the number.

If your total is now *0–7*, turn to **158**.
If it is *8* or more, turn to **11**.

179

You recognize the Black Cube to be a Nadziranim power crystal, an explosive device that can only be activated by creatures of the Darklands. Were you to take this item, it is possible that it could detonate and kill you at any time.

To continue, turn to **263**.

180

The missile is directly above the *Intrepid* when it explodes with a deafening roar. The blast slams you to the deck and, as you struggle to your feet, white-hot fragments of metal rain down upon you. Pick a number from the *Random Number Table* (in this instance 0 equals 10). The number you have picked represents the number of ENDURANCE points you have lost due to shrapnel wounds.

Amid the noise and chaos, you hear Captain Borse's strident voice, issuing commands to his shell-shocked crew. Despite the fearful blast, there are miraculously few casualties and the ship is soon brought under control. The topsails, ignited by the flash, are quickly cut away and jettisoned as the enemy vessels begin to close in for the kill. They turn to bring their weapons to bear, but the heavy, iron ships are slow and cumbersome, and, by the time they have changed formation, the *Intrepid* is out of range and sailing at speed into the dark waters of the Kaltesee.

Turn to **71**.

181

The explosion has caused havoc aboard the *Intrepid*. Men run howling across the decks, their clothes and hair ablaze, as swiftly the fire spreads throughout the ship. 'Save yourselves!' cries Davan. 'Abandon ship!'

You run to the deck rail, and, as you look along the beam, you see scores of men – Drakkarim and Sommlending alike – hurling themselves into the cold, dark waters of the Kaltesee rather than perish amid the roaring holocaust of flame.

If you possess the Magnakai Discipline of Hunt-mastery, Pathmanship, or Divination, turn to **4**.

If you possess none of these skills, turn to **224**.

182

The Giak wagon has drawn to a halt nearby, its driver and his companion eagerly awaiting the return of their escort. They are sniggering and discussing in detail all the hideous tortures they will inflict on you should the Drakkarim manage to capture you alive. So engrossed are they in their bloodthirsty talk that they fail to notice you creeping up on them until it is too late. Swiftly you silence the driver and turn in an instant to strike his companion. Miraculously, however, he manages to parry your blow on the shaft of his spear.

Giak Wagon-guard:
COMBAT SKILL 16   ENDURANCE 19

If you win the combat, turn to **335**.

183

The icy-cold winds blowing inland off the Kaltesee grow fiercer with every passing hour. Billowing black storm clouds mask the moon and plunge the land into an inky darkness that makes your search for shelter increasingly difficult. Only the steady flash of sheet lightning affords you any assistance. After three hours of fruitless search you resign yourself to spending a cold, wet, and throughly miserable night crouching at the bottom of a shallow gulley, with your cape pulled tent-like over your head to fend off the relentless rain. Owing to the cold, your fatigue and lack of sleep, your night in the open costs you 4 ENDURANCE points.

Turn to **300**.

184 – *Illustration XI*

As you follow the sycophantic creature along the corridor and up a flight of iron stairs to the deck level above, you ponder the name he called you – Cagath. No doubt it was the name of the Liganim whose identity you have taken on as a disguise. (Make a note of this name in the margin of your *Action Chart*. It could prove useful at a later stage of your adventure.)

A strange scene awaits you in the large, cylindrical chamber that is the gallery. At the centre of this steel hall, used by the Lajakeka's passengers as a meeting place and gambling den, there is a square pit some fifteen feet deep. On tiered seats that encircle the pit sit a motley group of creatures, some of whose features you recognize: Liganim, Nadziranim, Giak ore-masters, and a dozen or so whose origins are a mystery to you. They are all cheering or bawling obscenities at two bulky pit fighters, who are locked in hand-to-hand combat below. The fight ends abruptly with the beheading of one combatant, and the pit is cleared quickly whilst old bets are claimed and new ones are laid on the next bout. Into the gore-stained pit step two new fighters: an orange-skinned reptilian armed with a spiked club, and a blue-skinned humanoid

XI. An orange-skinned reptilian and a blue-skinned
humanoid step into the gore-stained pit

wielding a ball and chain. Giak crew pass along the tiers collecting bets. One of them appears at your side and tugs your sleeve. 'Ak nart gug?' he growls, waving a wad of orange and blue slips of hide, as he tries to tempt you to place a bet.

If you have any Kika and wish to bet on one of the pit fighters, turn to **61**.

If you do not possess any Kika, or do not wish to bet on the outcome of the fight, turn to **254**.

185

The limb wavers, then, hesitantly, it falls back to the edge of the abyss. With an arrow drawn to your lips you watch it retreat, your eye focused along the shaft at a point near the middle of the velvety black tendril. It continues to withdraw, then, as the tip is about to disappear from sight, there is a deafening screech. Suddenly a huge shape explodes from the crevasse, rising at such speed that its features are a blur. Instinctively you aim at the centre of this bulbous black form, and send your shaft whistling to meet its lightning-fast attack. The arrow strikes, and the creature screeches again − this time in pain.

You dive to the floor to avoid being hit by this howling horror, but it skims your scalp before slamming into the cavern wall. You glance back, expecting to see it slumped lifelessly on the floor, but to your surprise you see that it is still moving. Like a punctured balloon, it rebounds from the wall, then soars in a spiral towards the roof. There it is impaled on a cluster of stalactites that crack and give way under the impact of its vast weight. For a fleeting second you glimpse its ghastly features — its pear-shaped horny head and bulb-tipped antennae — before it plummets for the last time into the coal-black depths of the crevasse.

Turn to **87**.

186

Your senses tell you that the most vulnerable parts of the Xargath's head are its ears: the wall of the creature's skull is thinnest near the ear canals. Penetrate its ear with an arrow, and it could pass straight through the skull and enter its brain.

The Xargath roars and a gale of putrid breath tears at your face and clothing, forcing you away from the longboat. As you fight to stay on your feet, the beast bears down, tilting its head from side to side, revealing just a glimpse of your chosen target. Guided by instinct alone you raise your bow and fire.

Pick a number from the *Random Number Table* and add to it any bow skill bonuses to which you are entitled.

If your total is now *0–8*, turn to **313**.
If it is *9* or more, turn to **105**.

187

The rod is a Zejar-dulaga, a poisonous arrow imbued with magical accuracy. If you wish to turn off the power and take this Zejar-dulaga, mark it on your *Action Chart* as a Special Item, which you carry in your quiver.

188–190

Having satisfied yourself that there is nothing else of practical use in this laboratory, you decide to leave.

> If you wish to leave the laboratory by the door located behind the bench, turn to **54**.
>
> If you decide to re-enter the corridor and approach the guards, turn to **29**.

188

Your curiosity is aroused by the pouch of herbs you have discovered in the belt pouch of the dead Drakkar officer.

> If you have the Magnakai Discipline of Curing, or have reached the Kai rank of Principalin or more, turn to **145**.
>
> If you do not possess this skill, or have yet to attain this level of Kai training, turn to **201**.

189

Your attempts at deceiving this elite Drakkar warrior are met with a sneer of contempt. Cursing you as an imposter, he thrusts his spear at your face in an attempt to gouge out your tongue. You cannot evade combat and must fight your adversary to the death.

Death Knight Sentinel:
COMBAT SKILL 28   ENDURANCE 29

> If you win the fight, turn to **139**.

190

The howling makes the guard nervous — he shuffles uneasily and holds his iron stave defensively, as if expecting an attack at any moment. Yet, despite his alertness, he does not see you approaching until the very last moment, by which time it is too late to avoid your first blow. You deal him a grievous wound to the neck which sends him reeling, yet he recovers quickly and comes staggering towards you, his stave now ablaze with blue fire.

If possess the Sommerswerd, and wish to use it, turn to **208**.

If you do not possess this Special Item, or choose not to unsheathe it, turn to **289**.

191

After searching the ruins and finding nothing of practical use, you continue your lonely trek along the Argazad trail. For the most part, it runs parallel to the coast and is exposed to strong gusts of icy air that whip across the gulf. You find yourself having to lean into these sleet-tinged winds in order to remain upright. It is a tiring ordeal, and, as dusk begins to darken the sky, you welcome the chance to stop and rest.

You have just located a windproof niche in the lee of a rocky crag, and are about to settle down and rest, when you notice something moving towards you along the trail.

If you have the Magnakai Discipline of Huntmastery and have reached the Kai rank of Principalin or higher, turn to **251**.

If you do not possess this skill, or have yet to reach this level of Kai training, turn to **37**.

192

The Xargath roars like a demon, and a gale of blood-soaked breath whips your face and body, forcing you to lean into the blast in order to stay on your feet. The huge mouth descends, and your stomach churns when you see the grim remains of Sommlending sailors. Steeling yourself, you raise the sun-sword and prepare to strike out at the beast's ghastly maw.

Xargath: COMBAT SKILL 32   ENDURANCE 100

This creature is immune to Mindblast (but not Psi-surge).

If you win the combat, turn to **299**.

193

The screams of your pursuers grow louder with each passing second. Your pulse quickens and you release your arrow before you are sure of your target. The shaft arcs through the darkness and strikes the creature a glancing wound to his shoulder, causing him to yelp in pained surprise.

Fearful that his cry will alert those who are following you, you shoulder your bow hurriedly, draw a hand weapon, and run at the guard, grimly determined to finish him before he raises the alarm.

If you possess the Sommerswerd, and wish to use it to slay this creature, turn to **208**.
If you do not possess this Special Item, or choose not to unsheathe it, turn to **289**.

194

You hit the water with a mighty splash, and sink like a stone beneath the icy cold waves; yet the sudden shock serves to revive your battle-weary muscles and quickly you strike out for the surface. You emerge from the depths beside the hull of the enemy ironclad, which

is slowly pulling away from the wreck of the *Intrepid*.
The heads of the rivets, which protrude all along its
steel bow, offer a secure handhold for your numb
fingers and enable you to drag yourself on to the
shallow deck. You have barely caught your breath
when a Drakkar sailor, armed with a billhook, rushes
forward and lunges at your head.

Drakkar Sailor: COMBAT SKILL 19   ENDURANCE 24

Unless you possess the Magnakai Discipline of Huntmastery, reduce your COMBAT SKILL by 2 points for
the first round of this fight, owing to the surprise of
your enemy's attack.

If you win the combat, turn to **243**.

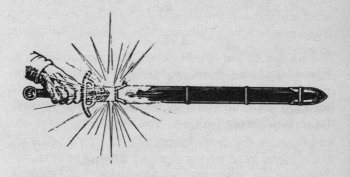

195

You slay the last of the deadly Crypt Spawn and stagger back, wiping their gore from your stinging eyes.
As your vision clears, to your horror you see Kraagenskûl bending over a bowl that rests on a plinth beside
his throne. It is filled with a silvery liquid, and at once
you recognize its purpose: it is a communicator, a
device through which he can converse with his leader,

Darklord Gnaag. The Sommerswerd has betrayed your identity, and Kraagenskûl is warning Gnaag of your presence here in Argazad.

With your heart pounding, you race across the chamber and kick the bowl from its plinth, destroying the image of Gnaag, that floats upon its shiny surface. Kraagenskûl screams in anger and lunges at your head, his sword now ablaze with tongues of black fire. You parry the blow and the two blades hiss furiously as their awesome power collides.

Darklord Kraagenskûl:
COMBAT SKILL 45   ENDURANCE 48

This being is immune to Mindblast (but not Psi-surge).

If you win the combat, turn to **318**.

196

The track and the stream wind their way towards a narrow gap in the Durncrag Range. Fixedly you stare at this gap. The longer you gaze, the more certain you are that it is a mountain pass, allowing the path to continue through to Argazad. You decide to press on and traverse the pass. Hopefully, the track will lead to the naval base where you can attempt to steal, or stow away on, some means of transport that will carry you to Argazad. The naval base must receive equipment from a Darkland city-fortress, and it is likely that Argazad is one such source of supply.

It is nearly dusk when the stony path reaches the narrow, boulder-strewn approach to the pass. It has been a long and tiring trek, yet in spite of your fatigue your senses warn you in good time of the danger that lies ahead. The pass is blocked by a wall and a stone watchtower, both guarded by Giak soldiers. Carefully you leave the path and creep along the bank of the stream, remaining hidden from view as slowly you edge your way nearer to the Giak outpost. An iron-banded gate in the centre of the wall allows traffic to use the pass, but it is closed and guarded by sentries. As dusk turns to darkness, you continue to observe every detail of the outpost and the surrounding mountains, in the hope of finding a way through.

If you wish to attempt to scale the wall, turn to **86**.

If you decide to avoid the outpost and search for an alternative route across the mountains, turn to **117**.

197

Fighting back your fear, you set off along the soot-encrusted street, keeping your head down and your shoulders forward to maintain your balance against the blasts of fiery wind that lash you mercilessly. At one corner, you happen upon a line of shallow pits, all filled with blazing oil. In the middle of each one is a pyramid of stone, festooned with chains, to which are manacled a dozen wretched creatures. They stand waist-deep in the flames, and, as they scream in pain, a group of Giaks amuse themselves by pushing them under with the hafts of their spears.

The Giaks are preoccupied with their cruel sport and you evade them easily. You continue along the street opposite the torture pits and arrive at a square flanked by four tall towers.

If you possess the Magnakai Discipline of Divination, and have reached the rank of Archmaster, turn to **124**.

(continued over)

If you do not possess this skill, or have yet to attain this level of Kai training, turn to **283**.

198

Using a Kai wrestling break to free yourself, you spin around and drive your clenched fist towards the face of your attacker. But before your blow connects with his chin, the ship gives a sudden lurch and you are both thrown to the floor. Your enemy lands on top of you and immediately closes his hands around your throat in an attempt to crush your windpipe.

Drakkar: COMBAT SKILL 21   ENDURANCE 26

Because of the situation, you are unable to draw a hand weapon and must fight this combat unarmed.

If you win the combat, turn to **253**.

199

The noise and fury of your combat alerts two guard patrols, one at either end of the corridor. They rush to investigate, and, when they see what you have done, they seal off the corridor and sound a general alarm. Within minutes, the tunnels are filled with snarling, snapping, screaming horrors. The guards then open the corridor and set them upon you.

You fight valiantly, slaying many before you are eventually overwhelmed and taken in chains before Darklord Gnaag. With cruel glee, he orders you to be cast into the Lake of Blood, where your endless suffering will feed its unholy flames for all eternity.

Tragically, your natural life and your mission end here.

It is nearing the hour of sunset when you set eyes on the naval base of Argazad. It nestles in the curve of a cliff – a natural harbour, protected from the pounding waters of the Helenag by a long promontory of rock. This wall-like barrier serves as a quay for more than fifty ironclad warships, the evil armada that is slowly strangling your country. Along the quay, huddled in the shadow of the surrounding cliffs, are a host of grim grey buildings, newly constructed from iron and stone. Their greasy windows flare with the orange light of fires that roar within, warming the Drakkarim sailors and marines who crew the Darklands' fleet.

Before entering the base, the trail joins a highway that approaches Argazad from the south. You stop to consult your map and discover that this road leads to the city-fortresses of Kaag and Aarnak. You consider avoiding the naval base and riding to Aarnak, but soon dismiss the idea. The journey would take you across the Naogizaga, one of the most desolate wastelands in all of Magnamund. Even if you could survive the heat, the dust, and the hellish creatures that dominate that grey desert, your mount would be sure to perish for lack of food and water.

A wall of stones, surmounted by an unbroken coil of razor-sharp wire, encircles the naval base. There is only one way through this perimeter wall – a gate that is guarded by a squad of Death Knights, the elite of the Drakkarim. Boldly you ride towards the gate, hoping to pass through unchallenged, but, as you approach, the Death Knights take up their spears and stand shoulder-to-shoulder across the road. 'Teg okak aga kog Argazad, shad?' demands their sergeant, gruffly.

If you possess the Magnakai Discipline of Psi-surge, and have reached the Kai rank of Principalin or more, turn to **17**.

If you have the Magnakai Discipline of Invisibility, and have reached the Kai rank of Scion-kai or more, turn to **167**.

If you possess neither of these skills and these ranks, turn to **314**.

201

The pungent aroma of the herbs, and their origin, makes you highly suspicious of their properties. Rather than risk swallowing them, you cast them aside and rise quickly to your feet. Confident that you have not overlooked any items that could possibly aid your mission, you decide that the time has come to leave.

Turn to **274**.

202

Greedily the sergeant snatches the coins from your hand (erase all the Kika from your *Action Chart*) and pockets them with a smile. Then he turns to his troops and shouts: 'Agna tok!'

To your relief they stand aside and you ride quickly through the gate. A shadowy street lies beyond, at the end of which there is a sign that indicates the way to the two main areas of Argazad: the ironclad harbour, and the supply depot.

If you wish to investigate the harbour, turn to **295**.

If you wish to investigate the supply depot, turn to **328**.

203

Your senses warn you that this creature has been summoned in Gnaag's defence. Its ghostly body is growing stronger every second, and you realize quickly that it is feeding on your fear. Drawing on your psychic reserves, you try to erect a mental barrier to prevent this psychic parasite from gorging on your fears.

Pick a number from the *Random Number Table*. If you have completed the Lore-circle of the Spirit, add 5 to the number you have picked.

If your total is now *0–6*, turn to **102**.
If it is 7 or more, turn to **114**.

204

'Fear can play strange tricks on your eyesight, comrade,' says the captain, in a patronizing tone. 'We'll be upon 'em soon enough. But we'll smell 'em long before we see 'em, mark my words.'

You try to convince him that you really can see the enemy but stubbornly he refuses to listen. Minutes later, the unmistakable stench of sulphur wafts across the deck and a shout rings out from the crow's nest that sends the crew into a frenzy of activity.

'Blockaders dead ahead!'

'Hard a-port!' bellows the captain, and frantically his helmsman spins the ship's wheel. The deck tilts steeply and the timbers groan their protest as the caravel veers away from the enemy line. To your right you see a Darkland ironclad less than a hundred yards distant, its steel-skinned deck bristling with formidable weaponry. Then a sudden flash of blue-white light illuminates its bow and a fiery projectile arcs across the sky towards the *Intrepid*.

Pick a number from the *Random Number Table*.

If the number you have picked is *0–2*, turn to **20**.
If the number is *3–9*, turn to **180**.

205

Using your powerful Kai skills to the full, you manage to prise the hideous, jelly-like creature from your head and hurl it to the floor. But no sooner has it hit the steel deck than it springs back at your face, forcing you to defend yourself.

Plaak: COMBAT SKILL 30   ENDURANCE 10

This creature is immune to Mindblast and Psi-surge.

If you win the combat, turn to **312**.

206

Your descent from the tunnel entrance to the base of the mountain is far more difficult than the climb up. Your ascent dislodged several sections of the trail, and the gaps that have appeared demand that you use all your skill and stamina to surmount them. One gap offers a ledge of crumbling rock no more than three inches wide on which to shuffle across. There are no handholds here; only the pressure of your chest and palms against the bare granite prevents you from falling.

Pick a number from the *Random Number Table*. If you have a rope, add 1 to the number you have picked.

If you possess the Magnakai Discipline of Huntmastery and have reached the Kai rank of Primate or more, add 2 to the number you have picked. If you have completed the Lore-circle of Solaris, add 3 to the number.

If your total score is now 0—4, turn to **62**.
If it is 5 or more, turn to **123**.

207

Your mastery of animals enables you to command the two seabirds to search elsewhere for food. Instantly they fly away, cawing their displeasure, leaving you free to paddle towards the shore.

Turn to **14**.

208

The moment you unsheathe the Sommerswerd, it radiates such goodly power that every creature in Helgedad is alerted to your presence. Within minutes you are surrounded by a nightmare legion of snarling, snapping, screaming horrors. You fight valiantly, and slay many before you are eventually overwhelmed and taken in chains before Darklord Gnaag. With cruel glee, he orders you to be cast into the Lake of Blood, where your endless suffering will feed its unholy flames for all eternity.

Tragically, your natural life and your mission end here.

209

With a swift and graceful movement, you snatch a dagger from the belt of one of your dead foes, spin on your heel, and fling it at the archer above before he has a chance to fire a third arrow. It sinks hilt-deep into his chest, sending him tumbling backwards into the black waters of the Kaltesee. With the stern deck now cleared of the enemy, you grab the helm and attempt to steer the ship away from the ironclad. The second enemy vessel is closing fast and you fear that the *Intrepid* will be smashed to driftwood if caught between the two.

Pick a number from the *Random Number Table*. For every Magnakai Discipline you possess above your initial three skills, add 1 to the number you have picked (for example, if you possess five Magnakai Disciplines, add 2 to the number you have picked).

If your total is now *0–9*, turn to **309**.
If it is *10* or more, turn to **151**.

210

Patiently, you watch the engineers complete their work. Then they climb down from the platform that services the tank area and leave the dry dock. When you are sure that the coast is clear, you climb the ladder to the tank and take a closer look at a control panel attached to its side. A dagger-sized length of white metal, suspended inside a thick glass tube, appears to control the power generated inside the orange tank. If you were to invert the tube, the change in position would be hard to detect but the result would be catastrophic. Once underway, the power would be allowed to build up unchecked and would eventaully cause the tank to explode.

If you possess the Magnakai Discipline of Divination, and have reached the Kai rank of Principalin or more, turn to **31**.

If you do not possess this skill, or have yet to attain this level of Kai training, you can invert the tube: turn to **345**.

Or, you can leave the tube untouched and abandon your sabotage attempt: turn to **223**.

211

Your keen eyes track the speeding bird and effortlessly you shoot it from the sky. It caws in pain and splashes into the sea less than an arm's length from your makeshift life-raft, enabling you to retrieve your arrow (you need not delete this arrow from your Weapons list).

Turn to **14**.

212

Your arrow strikes its target with chilling accuracy. The Drakkar throws his arms in the air and tumbles out of the saddle, killed instantly by your deadly shaft.

Turn to **79**.

213

With a fearful scream of vengeance, the Drakkar officer swings his scimitar down to cleave your neck in two. Skilfully you sidestep the blow and manage to turn the flashing blade with the edge of your weapon. He growls a curse and lunges again, determined to take your life.

Drakkar Marines Officer:
COMBAT SKILL 27   ENDURANCE 38

You can evade combat after two rounds: turn to **274**.

(continued over)

If you win the combat, turn to **232**.

214

You unsheathe the Sommerswerd and the shadowy chamber is flooded with blinding golden light, as if a sun had flared into being beneath its black dome. The steel walls vibrate, then buckle beneath an onslaught of pure energy that is radiating from the sword's blade. Until now the power of the the sun-sword has been held in check, locked and subdued within its divinely crafted blade. Even the surge of power that destroyed Darklord Zagarna at the walls of Holmgard was but a candle flicker compared to the searing radiance that is now pouring from its tip.

For an instant you see panic blaze madly in Gnaag's fly-like eyes, before he is consumed by the power of the Sommerswerd and vapourized to sightless atoms. With a cry of victory, you sheathe the sun-sword and stare at the place where, only seconds before, your arch-enemy confronted you.

Turn to **350**.

215

Using your advanced Kai skill you focus on a large, weed-draped boulder away to your left. The Giaks, led by their scout, rush towards it, their spears held at the ready. They cackle with glee at the thought of murdering another helpless Sommlending, but, of course, when they descend on the boulder, they discover that it conceals no one. The sound of their vile curses gradually fades as stealthily you escape along the beach.

Turn to **157**.

On a throne of hewn granite, ringed by seven pillars of fire, sits a being whose form radiates pure evil. A loose grey robe shrouds his skeletal frame. It is drawn closely about a stringy throat that swells and shrinks repulsively as he sucks the sulphurous air. With a claw-like finger, he scrapes nervously at the blistered flesh that is stretched tightly across the swollen left side of his face, attempting in vain to hook the head of a snake-like parasite that has burrowed into his jaw. His eyes, deep-sunken and red-rimmed with the unbearable pain of his affliction, burn with sick fanaticism as he listens impatiently to the pleas and excuses being offered by two who stand before him – the man in red and one other, both humbly bowed.

The luckless mortals plead their case, speaking in the Vassagonian tongue – a language that you mastered long ago. They speak of delays in the construction of a mighty battleship, of shortages of material and of too little time in which to finish their work. Their words anger the seated one. He curses them, and the floor shudders beneath the weight of his unnatural voice. 'You would dare defy me?' he roars. 'You would court the anger of Kraagenskûl, Lord of Argazad? Fools! Know you this. If your work is not completed before the next moon, you shall wish yourselves truly dead. A thousand years of agony shall be the reward for your failure, a thousand years of undeath in the dungeons of Helgedad!'

Fired by his own rage, the corpse-like Darklord Kraagenskûl, rises from his throne and draws the sword that hangs sheathed at his side. The blade is unlike any that you have seen. It is wholly black, a

XII. Darklord Kraagenskûl draws his sword

black so dense that it appears entirely separate from the hilt, like a tear through which you glimpse the nightmare depths of space. He levels the sword at the cowering men to reinforce his threat, but the blade rebels. It twists in his hand and points accusingly at the place where you are hiding. The Darklord narrows his feral eyes and a wave of psychic shock buffets your mind.

If you possess the Magnakai Discipline of Psi-screen, turn to **21**.

If you do not possess this skill, turn to **267**.

217

The Xargath sinks swiftly beneath the icy waters. Its tail breaks the surface and slaps the swirling foam, then it too is gone, trailing the creature's lifeless body as it spirals a hundred fathoms to its final resting place at the bottom of the Kaltesee.

An eerie silence descends upon the shattered decks of the *Intrepid* as the few who have survived the attack stare in horror at the swirling, blood-stained sea. Then begin the cries of the injured, and those who are still able to stand begin the grim task of recovering bodies and staunching wounds. You help with the search and find Captain Borse lying near the ship's longboat. He is unconscious and badly injured: both his legs have been broken at the thigh by one swipe of the monster's tail. You attempt to revive him with your basic Kai healing skills, but he is in deep shock and does not respond.

If you possess the Magnakai Discipline of Curing, turn to **159**.

If you do not possess this skill, turn to **41**.

218

The creature falls limply to the floor as your killing blow slices it almost in two. Curious as to what manner of beast it was you lift back its sundered folds of rubbery grey flesh with the tip of your weapon and notice two sets of snake-like fangs, both still oozing a sticky yellow fluid. Your senses tell you that this fluid is deadly venom, capable of killing a victim in seconds. Whoever placed this Plaak in your cabin was attempting to assassinate you.

Disgusted by the smell of the creature, you flick its remains under your bunk. As you are rising to your feet, you hear a loud, intermittent whistle sounding on the deck above: it is the signal that Helgedad has been sighted by the lookout. With your heart pounding at the thought of seeing the Darklord's most infamous stronghold for the first time, you leave your cabin and ascend to the deck above.

Turn to **326**.

219

You understand enough of the Giak language to know that the enemy captain is preparing to hasten the *Intrepid* to the bottom of the sea. The metallic tube is the means by which the ironclads launch their fire-missiles, one of which you have already encountered when running the blockade out of Toran. This one is loaded and is being aimed directly at the waterline of the *Intrepid*. At first it strikes you as a wasteful attack: the *Intrepid* is sinking so fast that to fire upon it now seems to serve no practical purpose. Then you realize what the enemy commander is planning, and the thought of it makes your blood boil.

Turn to **113**.

220

Despite the loss of your protective amulet, your highly advanced Kai skills prevent the burning temperature and poisonous atmosphere of Helgedad from causing you permanent harm. You do, however, suffer in the short term, while your body adjusts to the new environment: lose 2 ENDURANCE points.

Turn to **280**.

221

With surprising grace, the Zlanbeast glides smoothly to a halt atop the building. The air wafting from the estuary reeks of iron and soot, and, as you jump down from the saddle, you discover that the roof is covered with a layer of grey dust several inches thick.

The screech of a rusty hinge alerts you to an opening trapdoor. The grey and ugly face of an angry Giak soldier appears. He clambers on to the roof and begins shouting at you, demanding that you explain how you came to be in possession of a Zlanbeast, a creature used only by the Darklords and their undead lieutenants.

If you wish to ignore his threats and demand that he take you to the Slavemaster, turn to **281**.

If you have any Kika, and wish to offer them to the Giak as a bribe, in return for his help in finding the Slavemaster, turn to **108**.

222

Half-blinded by dust and darkness, you drag yourself out from beneath a tangled mass of bodies and broken timbers, and stagger drunkenly towards an opening in the wall of the ship's hold. Beyond it a narrow corridor leads to a stair, where one of the crew lies dead, sprawled face-upwards, his hands locked around the blade of the Drakkar dagger that claimed his life. Still dazed by the fall, your senses fail to alert you to an enemy who is lurking in the shadows. You are about to set foot on the stairs when he attacks, seizing you from behind and holding you in a powerful neck lock.

If you possess the Magnakai Discipline of Invisibility, and have reached the Kai rank of Scion-kai or more, turn to **32**.

If you do not possess this skill, or have yet to reach this level of Kai training, turn to **198**.

223

A group of Drakkarim, led by a figure dressed in a hooded red robe, is making its way towards the ironclad. Suddenly it halts and one of the Drakkar warriors points at the platform on which you are standing. Rather than stay and confront them, you slide down the ladder quickly and slip away under cover of the piles of steel plates and girders.

By the time the group reaches the platform, you are back on your horse and heading along the street that leads away from the dock.

Turn to **97**.

224

Your Kai sixth sense screams a warning that you are about to be attacked. You spin on your heel to see a Drakkar marine lunging towards you with a stiletto-bladed dagger gripped tightly in his blistered hand.

Drakkar Marine: COMBAT SKILL 19   ENDURANCE 23

This adversary is immune to Mindblast (but not Psi-surge). Owing to the speed of his attack, you are unable to evade combat or draw a weapon until the beginning of the third round.

If you wish to evade combat at the third round, you can do so by leaping overboard into the sea: turn to **58**.

If you win the combat, turn to **91**.

225

Once the bets have been collected, all eyes turn to the pit-master who will strike the gong that begins the combat. But the combat is over before it begins officially. The orange-skinned creature suddenly springs at his opponent and slams his spiked club down on his unprotected skull, killing him instantly. The crowd hoots with glee at the beast's display of low cunning, and despite some loud protests by those who, like you, bet on the humanoid, the pit-master reluctantly declares the reptilian the winner.

Erase all the Kika you staked and turn to **134**.

226 – *Illustration XIII (overleaf)*

The black tendril retreats — it is as if the creature can sense that you pose a threat to its safety — until it is hovering directly above the abyss. You step forward, intending to hasten it on its way, when suddenly a huge shape explodes from the crevasse, rising at such speed that its features are just a blur. The creature emits

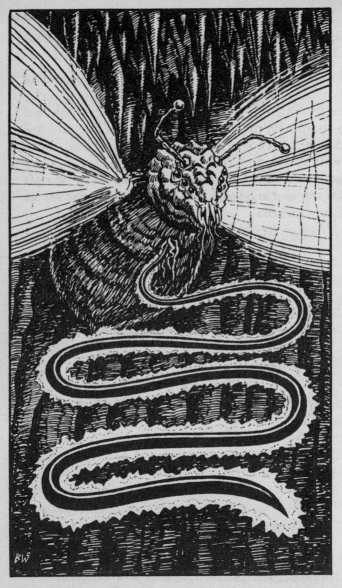

XIII. The Ictakko's tendril skims your shoulder

a deafening screech then dives straight towards your chest.

Instinctively you drop to the floor to avoid being hit by this howling horror, but, as it streaks past your body, its tendril skims your shoulder. There is a flash and a sharp pain runs down your arm; the creature has discharged a bolt of electrical energy that leaves your arms numb and nerveless — lose 3 ENDURANCE points. Gritting your teeth against the pain, you get to your feet in time to see the creature swooping for a second time.

Ictakko: COMBAT SKILL 25   ENDURANCE 35

Unless you possess the Magnakai Discipline of Nexus and have reached the Kai rank of Archmaster, you must lose an extra 1 ENDURANCE point every time this creature inflicts a wound during the combat, owing to the numbing effect of its electrical attack.

If you win the combat, turn to **343**.

227

Your skill and dexterity make scaling the wall an easy task. You reach the parapet, climb over, then slip stealthily down the other side without being seen by either the guards in the watchtower, or the two on the wall. Then, hiding behind the rocks and crags that line the roadway, you escape through the pass, undetected.

Turn to **137**.

228

Roughly you turn over the bodies of your slain enemies, and search through their pockets and packs.

229

You discover the following items, which may be of use to you during your mission:

> DAGGER
> SWORD
> AXE
> SHORT SWORD
> 40 KIKA (equivalent to 4 Gold Crowns)
> BLANKET
> BLACK KEY

If you wish to keep any of these items, remember to adjust your *Action Chart* accordingly.

To continue along the tunnel, turn to **280**.

229

You pass the time prior to your departure resting and reviewing the mission in fine detail. Eventually the hour of your leaving arrives and Banedon and Rimoah escort you to Toran harbour and see you safely aboard the caravel *Intrepid*. Before they disembark, Banedon hands you a sealed envelope and a Golden Amulet on a chain.

'Wear this for your protection,' he says, as he fastens the chain around your neck. 'It will keep you safe from the heat and poisonous atmospheres that pervade your destination.' (Mark the Golden Amulet on your *Action Chart* as a Special Item — you need not discard another item in its favour if you already carry the maximum quota.)

'And the envelope?' you say, quizzically.

'Neither Captain Borse, nor his volunteer crew, are aware of your identity or the vital nature of your voyage. All they know is that they are expected to break through the blockade and carry you safely to Durenor. When you are clear of the enemy, hand this envelope to the captain. It contains his new orders to steer a course for the Aarnak Estuary. He is a fine captain: you can trust in his skill and the bravery of his crew to see you through the dangerous waters of the Kaltesee.'

Moments later the captain emerges from his cabin. A grey and grizzled old seaman, he sports a leather cloak that swings easily from his broad, muscular shoulders. He welcomes you aboard with a ready smile and firm handshake, then excuses himself in order to supervise the final preparations for the voyage. 'May the gods Kai and Ishir watch over you, Lone Wolf,' whispers Lord Rimoah, as he and Banedon make ready to disembark, 'and grant us a lasting victory over the forces of darkness.'

Turn to **325**.

230

Wielding a weapon of the Darklords, you strike Taktaal a grievous blow that wounds him deeply. Shrieking an unearthly cry of pain, he retreats from the Transfusor and unhooks a mace, carved from a solid chunk of black crystal, from a chain around his putrescent neck. As he raises it, you move forward to strike again.

Darklord Taktaal (wounded):
COMBAT SKILL 36   ENDURANCE 40

This supernatural being is immune to Mindblast (but not Psi-surge).

If you win the combat, turn to **78**.

231

You take aim and fire at the leading Drakkar, sending your shaft spinning deep into his leather-clad chest. He screams, his cry muffled by his battle-mask, and crumples to his knees. The remaining three Drakkar press home their attack. Quickly they advance, and you barely have time to unsheathe a hand weapon before they are upon you, screaming their bloodthirsty cries of revenge.

Drakkarim Escorts:
COMBAT SKILL 23   ENDURANCE 30

If you win the combat, turn to **182**.

232

The Drakkar gurgles his death cry and falls heavily to the deck, his scimitar still clasped firmly in his hand. Then the first of his troops appear at the rail. For a moment they hesitate when they see their officer lying dead, but shock soon turns to fury. 'Shez dot got!' they scream, as they thunder towards you, murder blazing in their cruel eyes.

If you wish to evade their attack, turn to **274**.
If you decide to stand your ground and receive their attack, turn to **347**.

233

Desperately you try to shake off the clammy creature, but it manages to sink two sets of snake-like fangs into your neck and inject its deadly venom.

If you possess the Magnakai Discipline of Curing, and have reached the Kai rank of Mentora or more, turn to **136**.

If you do not possess this skill, or have yet to reach this level of Kai training, turn to **73**.

234

Although the cave is empty, you detect the lingering scent of a creature that has slept here in the last twenty-four hours. If this is the creature's lair, it is likely to return to seek shelter from the storm.

If you wish to leave the cave and look for shelter elsewhere, turn to **183**.

If you decide to stay in the cave and remain on your guard in case its previous occupant should return, turn to **18**.

235

'The Transfusor, which you must destroy to ensure the end of the Darklords who are now outside the boundaries of this realm, is located in the uppermost chamber of the Tower of the Damned. You will find this tower in a part of the city known as the Imperial Sector. But be warned! This sector is the most heavily guarded area of the city, for it is here that Gnaag himself resides.'

The Slavemaster takes a strange mask from a nearby table and offers it to you. It is made of a green, glass-like mineral and is shaped into a hideous visage. 'Wear this always. It will keep safe your identity from any casual inspection.' You accept the Green Mask (mark this as a Special Item on your *Action Chart* — you need not discard any other item in its favour if you already hold the maximum), and listen carefully as the Slavemaster concludes your briefing.

Turn to **293**.

236

You release the bow string and send the arrow whistling deep into the Xargath's cavernous mouth, causing the monster to twist its head and hiss like a steam vent. But still it advances undeterred. Cursing your misfortune, you shoulder your bow and draw a hand weapon in readiness for its impending attack.

Turn to **344**.

237

You crash down upon the Drakkar and wrench him from his saddle, but you cannot keep a firm grip on his shiny leather armour, and you hit the ground with a jolt that leaves you breathless: lose 1 ENDURANCE point.

Turn to **175**.

238

Swiftly you unshoulder your bow and draw the magical arrow to your lips. Its glowing shaft betrays the power that is locked within it, a power that can kill those who created and harnessed it to murder others. Taktaal senses that his doom is near and tries to give vent to a cry of alarm, but the cry dies in his throat as you send the Zejar-Dulaga burrowing deep into his evil heart. With a surge of incredible strength, Taktaal drags the arrow from his body and collapses at the edge of the dais. A foul black gas hisses from the gaping wound and his body dissolves rapidly and fades until all that is left is a dull grey stain on the shiny black steel floor.

'Ghanesh will be proud of you!' comes a voice from the shadows, full of malevolence. It is a sound that strikes terror in your heart, for immediately you recognize the rasping tone of your most hated foe – Darklord Gnaag.

Turn to **50**.

239

You draw a weapon and leap forward, determined to prevent the slaughter of your defenceless companions. The speed and ferocity of your attack takes the captain and his two gunners completely by surprise. With deadly speed you dispatch the enemy commander and one of his men, then turn to parry a sword thrust from the remaining gunner. He screams maniacally as he tries to cut you down.

Drakkarim Gunner:
COMBAT SKILL 19   ENDURANCE 25

If you win and the fight lasts three rounds or less, turn to **272**.

If you win and the combat lasts four rounds or more, turn to **155**.

240

Your killing blow draws a howl from Darklord Kraagenskûl, so loud that it shakes the very foundations of the building. He falls, yet as he does so, his withered frame vanishes before your eyes, leaving only a tattered grey robe and a black sword to mark his passing.

If you wish to keep Helshezag, the sword of Darklord Kraagenskûl, mark it on your *Action Chart* as a Special Item. (You wrap this sword in the remains of the Darklord's grey robe and carry it vertically, tied behind your backpack.) When used in combat, it will add 5 points to your COMBAT SKILL, and 7 points when used against a Darklord of Helgedad. However, prolonged use of this evil blade will weaken your ENDURANCE score. In the second and subsequent rounds of every combat in which you use the sword, you must reduce your ENDURANCE level by 1 point.

Having recovered from your combat, you quickly leave the chamber by a stair that leads to the roof. There you discover the Zlanbeast, Kraagenskûl's personal winged mount, perched on a raised log. Standing nearby is a Death Knight armed with a spear, staring absent-mindedly over the parapet at the harbour lights below. The Zlanbeast sniffs the air and shuffles along its perch with a nervous, rolling gait. It senses that you are its natural enemy and it is becoming agitated in your presence. You must act quickly and with skill if you are to use this beast to escape from Argazad.

If you wish to approach the Death Knight and tell him that he is wanted at the barracks, turn to **92**.

If you wish to creep up on the warrior and launch a surprise attack, turn to **178**.

If you have a bow and wish to use it, turn to **310**.

241

For two days and nights the *Intrepid* forges a course through stormy waters, running ahead of a chill wind that sweeps down from the glaciers of Kalte in the north. The sea becomes increasingly hazardous, with sleet squalls and lightning storms that break without warning. Yet the dawn of the third day heralds a sudden change in the weather: fog. A windless, soundless, grey, forbidding damp that cuts off eyesight at an arm's length and leaves the crew soaked and shivering. Many stare enviously at your Kalkoth hide cloak as they attend to their early-morning duties in quiet discomfort.

'Curse this fog,' grumbles Captain Borse, staring helplessly at the clammy mist that holds his ship becalmed. 'Better a gale or a kuri-storm than this.' For countless hours the ship lies dormant, rocking gently on the cold, listless sea. Staring at the wall of fog, it is easy to imagine all manner of creatures lurking within. The eerie silence does little to allay the superstitious fears of the crew, and when suddenly the quiet is disturbed by a shoal of red-finned sea carp, more than one man cries out in shocked surprise.

If you possess the Magnakai Discipline of Animal Control, turn to **305**.

If you do not possess this skill, turn to **60**.

242

With the hellish cries of the minions of Darklord Taktaal ringing in your ears, you flee for your life along a dark and twisting alley. The surface is ankle-deep in stinking carrion, which makes keeping your balance a difficult task, but the fear of what will befall you should you slip is all that you need to ensure that you stay on your feet. The alley ends at a wider street running from north to south. The sound of howling wolves dissuades you from turning north, so you set off quickly along the street that heads towards the southern sectors of the city.

Pick a number from the *Random Number Table*. If you have the Magnakai Discipline of Pathsmanship, and have reached the Kai rank of Mentora or more, add 5 to the number you have picked.

If your total is now *0–6*, turn to **120**.
If it is 7 or more, turn to **173**.

243

The force of your killing blow sends the Drakkar reeling backwards across the deck. He collides with another sailor, who was coming to his aid, and knocks him headlong into the sea. You brace yourself in case there is another waiting to rush at you, but the smoke from the vessel's funnel is so thick, and the other Drakkarim are so preoccupied with hooking their marines out of the water, that they fail to notice you creeping towards the wheelhouse near the middle of the deck. A steel door swings open at your approach and three hefty Drakkarim confront you on the threshold. You parry one's blade, take the second in the chest, and see the third spin sideways, trailing scarlet spray from the fatal wound you have dealt him. A quick thrust to the heart puts paid to the remaining sailor. He screams and falls through the doorway, tumbling down an iron staircase that descends into noise-filled darkness.

If you have the Magnakai Discipline of Divination, turn to **26**.

If you do not possess this skill, you can either descend the stairs: turn to **266**.

Or you can slam shut the steel door and look for another place to hide from the Drakkarim sailors on deck: turn to **169**.

244

Sparks of brilliant light dance wildly before your eyes as the power of Kraagenskûl's attack sears the fabric of your mind. You reel under the onslaught yet manage, in your desperation, to repulse the assault: lose 4 ENDURANCE points. As the shock slowly fades and your vision returns to normal, you steel yourself to face the Darklord once more.

Turn to **147**.

245

Your arrow soars into the sky, missing the bird by a hand's breadth, and, in your rush to draw a hand weapon, carelessly you drop your bow into the sea (erase this weapon from your *Action Chart*). Cursing the loss of your weapon, you get ready to defend yourself against this air attack.

Turn to **268**.

246

You drag the dead Liganim into the shadows and check his pockets for anything that may prove useful. All that you discover is a Black Key. If you wish to keep this key, mark it on your *Action Chart* as a Backpack Item.

To continue, turn to **130**.

247

As your hand closes on the hilt, a voice in your head screams a warning. You recall the words of Lord Rimoah when, in the Externment Chamber of the Magician's Guild of Toran, he gave you the special korlinium scabbard that now sheathes the sun-sword: 'Remember, to unsheathe the Sommerswerd within the Darklands is to light a beacon of warning that Gnaag will surely see . . .'

Rather than draw the sword and risk the failure of your mission, you withdraw your hand as the Giaks launch their attack.

Giak Sentries: COMBAT SKILL 17   ENDURANCE 22

You must fight the first two rounds of this combat unarmed.

> You are able to evade combat at the start of the third round by leaping from the battlements: turn to **96**.
> If you win the combat, turn to **349**.

248

You leap over the body of your slain enemy and rush to help Davan, who is being driven back across the

deck by three snarling Drakkarim. 'For Sommerlund!'
you cry, as you launch your attack, felling two of his
adversaries with a single, sweeping blow. Deftly he
puts paid to the third, and together you advance
towards the stern where the enemy are attempting to
capture the helm. Already several of the crew lie
bleeding on the deck, and, although they fight bravely,
they are no match for the vicious Drakkarim marines.

At the foot of the makeshift stairs that ascend to the
stern deck, you are confronted by the leader of the
enemy's assault team. 'Okak gaz egor!' he growls, his
evil eyes glinting through the slits in his studded leather
battle-mask. 'Shez ok okak nogjat ash gajog ok okak
adez!' With that, he lifts his reddened axe and strides
forward to meet your advance.

Drakkarim Marine Sergeant:
COMBAT SKILL 26   ENDURANCE 30

You can evade combat after the first two rounds:
turn to **7**.
If you win the combat, turn to **290**.

249

You ignore the group and follow a handful of noisy
Giak crew members, in the hope of overhearing
something that gives you a clue as to the whereabouts
of the Imperial Sector of Helgedad. The tunnel soon
joins another at a point where a granite staircase
ascends to the surface. The crew climb the stairs, and
you watch them disappearing through an open archway that gives access to the street above. What should
you do now?

If you possess the Magnakai Discipline of Pathsmanship, and have reached the Kai rank of Tutelary or more, turn to **83**.

If you do not possess this skill, or have yet to reach this level of Kai training, turn to **67**.

250

While you languish in the cell, the Death Knight sergeant conveys your equipment to his commander, Darklord Kraagenskûl. At once he recognizes their origins and deduces your true identity. Word is sent to Gnaag, and within the space of four short hours he journeys to the naval base from the city of Helgedad. He orders you to be executed at the earliest opportunity and demands, on pain of death, that the task be accomplished successfully.

It is Darklord Kraagenskûl who suggests the method for your execution, and the irony of it appeals greatly to his master. At dawn, the Crystal Explosive that you had intended to use in Helgedad, is placed next to the door of the cell. The barracks are evacuated and the explosive is primed. Fifteen minutes later, your life and your mission are brought to an abrupt and final end.

251

Using your telescopic vision, you focus on the approaching shape and, as it draws nearer, you are able to discern exactly what it is. You see a wagon laden with barrels and boxes, and drawn by six oxlike creatures. Two Giaks are sitting on top of the wagon: the driver, who is lashing the team with a whip, and a guard, who appears to be fast asleep. Behind the wagon are four horsemen – Drakkarim escorts, judging by their size and the cut of their black leather armour.

Their route will take them close to where you are sheltering. Mindful of the Giak ability to see in the dark, you decide to stay in hiding and wait for them to pass.

Turn to **304**.

252

The angry screams of the Giak search party fill the night sky. The Giaks witnessed the slaying of their comrades and are now rushing forward to kill you in turn. Aching with the fatigue of your exertions, you choose to evade rather than fight the remaining enemy, and begin the steep climb towards the cliff top.

Halfway up the cliff you make out some shadows descending the path ahead. You sense that it is another Giak search party attempting to cut you off and your pulse quickens. You look for a way to avoid them, but the only escape from the path is a sheer drop to the beach below.

If you possess the Magnakai Discipline of Hunt-mastery, turn to **30**.

If you do not possess this skill, turn to **132**.

253

Wiping the sweat and grime from your eyes, you clamber up the stairs and emerge on the stern deck, close to the helm. There you find Davan and a hand-ful of the crew fighting a desperate mêlée against a determined enemy who outnumber them by two to one. You raise your weapon and cleave a path towards your beleaguered allies. As you draw closer, Davan sees you and gives a cheer. You acknowledge his shout with your battle-cry, 'For Sommerlund!'

He replies, but this time with a cry of warning: 'Archer above you!'

You glance up into the rigging, and a cold spike of fear stabs your heart as you glimpse the gloating face of a Drakkar. With one hand he holds a bow and with the other he draws back an arrow to his bristle-bearded chin. He mouths a curse and lets fly his deadly shaft.

Pick a number from the *Random Number Table*. If you have the Magnakai Discipline of Huntmastery, add 2 to the number you have picked. If you have completed the Lore-circle of the Spirit, add 3 to the number.

If your total is now *0–3*, turn to **122**.
If it is *4–7*, turn to **53**.
If it is *8* or more, turn to **321**.

254

All the bets are quickly placed and the pit-master prepares to start the proceedings, but the fight is over almost as soon as it begins. Without waiting for the pit-master to hammer the gong that signifies the start of combat, the orange-skinned fighter springs across the pit and buries its spiked club between the startled eyes of its opponent, killing him instantly. The crowd hoots with glee at the beast's display of low cunning, and, despite some loud protests by those who bet on the humanoid, the pit-master reluctantly declares the reptilian the winner.

Bets are about to be placed on the next round of combat when a loud, intermittent whistle interrupts the preliminaries: it is the signal that Helgedad has been sighted by the lookout. Some of the crowd leave their seats in order to view the Black City through the tiny portholes that line the walls of the gallery. With your heart pounding at the thought of seeing the Darkland's most infamous stronghold for the first time, you leave the pit and join them.

Turn to **326**.

255

Kraagenskûl watches you step over the gore-stained bodies of his creations, then raises his black sword as you approach him boldly. 'Here lies your doom, fool!' he roars, waving his sword before his ghastly face. 'Come. Take it . . . if you dare!'

Cautiously you circle the Darklord, taking care to remain beyond the reach of his sorcerous blade, but he moves towards you with surprising speed. As you dive to avoid his attack, you seek a chance to turn the odds a little in your favour. With a mighty kick, you send one of the fiery pillars toppling towards your foe. He screams and dodges aside, but the column glances his shoulder as it slams to the granite floor with a crackling roar. The black sword spins from his hand and slides to a halt near the base of the throne. For a moment your eyes meet, then simultaneously you race to retrieve the blade.

Pick a number from the *Random Number Table*. For every Magnakai Discipline that you possess, including your initial three skills, add 1 to the number you have picked.

If your total is now *0–5*, turn to **90**.
If it is *6* or more, turn to **133**.

256

You stand at the ship's rail and stare at the surrounding wall of darkness. The salty air is cold upon your face, but, as you breathe deeply, you detect a strangely bitter smell, like burnt sulphur, being carried on the wind. You are about to mention this to the captain when a shout rings out from the crow's nest that sends the crew into a frenzy of activity. 'Blockaders dead ahead!'

'Hard a-port!' bellows the captain, and his helmsman spins the ship's wheel frantically.

Five Darkland ironclads loom into view. They each carry a formidable array of weapons mounted on their steel-skinned decks, and protruding from the middle of each craft is a tall funnel, which belches forth a cloud of choking, sulphurous smoke. As the *Intrepid* swerves to avoid collision, this acrid smoke wafts across the water and engulfs the crew, causing them to cough and retch violently.

Suddenly, a flash of blue-white light illuminates the bow of the nearest ironclad and a fiery projectile arcs across the sky.

Pick a number from the *Random Number Table*.

If the number you have picked is *0–1*, turn to **20**.
If it is *2–9*, turn to **180**.

257

The leathery Zlanbeast flaps its wings and shifts its weight uneasily from one clawed foot to the other. Carefully you approach this dangerous creature, with your eyes fixed upon its saddle and your nerves on edge, fearing that at any moment it will slash you with its razor-hooked beak.

Pick a number from the *Random Number Table*. If you possess the Magnakai Discipline of Animal Control, and have reached the Kai rank of Archmaster or more, add 4 to this number.

If your total is now *0–4*, turn to **333**.
If it is *5* or more, turn to **112**.

258

Starbursts of light flash before your eyes and the pain in your head grows ever more unbearable until you feel sure that your skull is about to explode: lose 8 ENDURANCE points. (If you possess either a Psychic Ring *or* a Grey Crystal Ring, lose only 3 ENDURANCE points.)

Then, unexpectedly, the pain stops and Taktaal shrieks with anger and surprise. He has seen through your disguise and your true identity shocks him to the core.

Turn to **176**.

259

Your first arrow pierces a heart, but your second is deflected by a steel breastplate. Before you have a chance to fire again, the surviving gunner is upon you, his short sword unsheathed and ready to stab at your chest.

Drakkar Gunner:
COMBAT SKILL 19   ENDURANCE 25

Unless you possess the Magnakai Discipline of Huntmastery, you must fight the first two rounds of combat unarmed.

If you win and the fight lasts three rounds or less, turn to **272**.

If you win and the combat lasts four rounds or more, turn to **155**.

260 – *Illustration XIV*

The Slavemaster dons a mask that covers his nose and mouth, through which he is able to breath safely the noxious air that swirls outside his tower. He takes you to the outskirts of Aarnak in his personal chariot, to a vast, open-cast quarry. The means of your transportation to Helgedad waits at the edge of the quarry's vast crater. Your jaw opens in amazement when you set eyes on the vehicle, for it is gigantic, by far the largest vehicle you have ever seen on dry land.

'It is a Lajakeka, a "stone-taker",' says the Slavemaster, clearly amused by your awed reaction to this wheeled leviathan. 'It is filled with ore, mined here at this crater, that is destined for the furnaces of Helgedad. You are to be a passenger on its return journey to the Black City. However, you will not be travelling alone. There are several Liganim, and some others besides, who will be fellow travellers. Be wary of them and remember all that I have said.'

XIV.   The Lajakeka waits at the edge of the quarry's crater

Then he bids you farewell, and watches as you climb the wide ramp that leads into the belly of the steel beast. Inside it is not unlike a ship, with cabins for the travellers and crew, and interconnecting passages that service the vast cargo holds full of ore. Giak crew allocate cabins at random, and once you are safely inside yours, you pull the drawbolt and try to make yourself comfortable on an unpadded steel bunk. Then the screech of metal on metal and the dull throbbing of the Lajakeka's engines fill your ears. The bunk shudders and your pulse quickens: your journey to Helgedad is underway.

You have been travelling for less than an hour when you hear a knock on your cabin door.

> If you possess the Magnakai Discipline of Divination, and have reached the Kai rank of Mentora or more, turn to **298**.
>
> If you do not possess this skill, or have yet to reach this level of Kai training, and wish to open your cabin door, turn to **85**.
>
> If you do not possess this skill or have yet to reach this level of Kai training and wish to ignore the knock, turn to **144**.

261

The Darklord laughs and the chamber vibrates to the sound of his ghastly glee.

'So, the worm-master's minion wishes to serve a lord with true power, does he? Very well, you treacherous slime, but first you will have to prove yourself worthy of my lordship.'

He moves towards the Transfusor, in doing so turning his back on you.

If you wish to take this opportunity to launch a surprise attack at the Darklord, turn to **176**.
If you do not wish to attack him, turn to **168**.

262

Before you can thank the captain for his generosity, he lapses into a merciful unconsciousness that spares him the pain of his injuries. Having done what you can to make him comfortable, you return to the deck to survey the damage.

Over half the crew have been killed or injured in the attack and the ship herself is badly mauled. The main mast is down, the sails hang in tatters, and there is a gaping hole that stretches along the port beam to within a few feet of the waterline.

'We can patch up the canvas and work the ship on a skeleton crew,' says Davan, peering over the splintered rail, 'but if we catch a storm this far out to sea, we're all done for.'

Turn to **330**.

263

You pause just long enough to drag the dead guard's body into the shadows, then slip quickly into the tower. A semi-circular passageway opens on to a hall, where a wide steel staircase descends to a torchlit passage. Cautiously you proceed, poised to react to the slightest sound. You hear nothing: the stair and the passage beyond it appear deserted.

Turn to **130**.

264 – *Illustration XV*

You aim and fire at a point between the creature's yellow, cat-like eyes. The shaft strikes, but the beast has already begun to leap and it misses its vital target, sinking instead into a slab of muscle that sheathes its neck. It shrieks when it hits the ground, which shudders beneath the vast stone weight. Quickly you shoulder your bow and move forward to finish the beast before it can recover, but as you make your attack, you discover that the creature is ready to receive it.

Egorgh: COMBAT SKILL 24   ENDURANCE 30

This creature is particularly susceptible to psychic attack; double all bonuses you would normally be entitled to if using Mindblast or Psi-surge during this combat.

If you win the combat, turn to **153**.

265

The fight is over almost as soon as it begins. Without waiting for the pit-master to hammer the gong that signifies the start of combat, the orange-skinned fighter springs across the pit and buries its spiked club between the startled eyes of its opponent, killing him instantly. The crowd hoots with glee at the beast's display of low cunning, and, despite some loud protests by those who bet on the humanoid, the pit-master reluctantly declares the reptilian winner.

Double the amount of Kika you staked and make the necessary adjustments to your *Action Chart*.

Turn to **134**.

XV.   The huge, shaggy Egorgh gets ready to leap at your chest

266

You have taken less than a dozen steps into the black and humid depths, when you glimpse movement below and hear the sound of angry Drakkarim voices: the dead sailor has been discovered. The slick hiss of steel drawn from leather warns you that the crew are about to ascend the stairs. They are enraged and determined to avenge the death of their companion.

If you possess a Fireseed and wish to use it, turn to **302**.

If you decide to avoid a confrontation on the stairs, turn to **169**.

If you choose to draw a weapon and prepare to defend yourself, turn to **68**.

267

A blinding pain engulfs your mind. It distorts your vision and drags you screaming to your knees. In desperation, you claw at your scalp and plead for the agony to cease: lose 8 ENDURANCE points.

As if in answer to your plea, the pain disappears. But your fear remains and grows deeper as you stare into the merciless eyes of Darklord Kraagenskûl.

Turn to **147**

268

The bird streaks towards you at such a speed that instinctively you know that your first blow must count. There will be no time for a second before its dagger-sharp beak rakes your face.

Sea-scavenger: COMBAT SKILL 22   ENDURANCE 10

The creature is immune to Mindblast (but not Psi-surge). If the number of ENDURANCE points you lose in the first round of combat is greater than the number lost by your enemy, then the creature's attack has caused lasting injury to your eyesight, and any subsequent ENDURANCE points that you may lose during the combat are **permanent** (they reduce your basic ENDURANCE score and cannot be restored through the use of healing, potions, etc).

If you win the combat, turn to **14**.

269

The sergeant snatches the Medal from your hand and scrutinizes it with greedy eyes. Slowly he nods his head, then turns to face his troops. 'Agna tok!' he commands. 'Dok lug shad!'

You breathe a silent sigh of relief as they begin to move aside. Then you slap your horse's rump and urge him through the gate. A shadowy street lies beyond, at the end of which is a sign that indicates the way to the two main areas of Argazad: the ironclad harbour and the supply depot.

If you wish to investigate the harbour, turn to **295**.

If you wish to investigate the supply depot, turn to **328**.

270

You load and take aim at the beast's massive head, as it swings low across the deck, smashing and crushing all before it. Its scaly hide looks as tough as steel plate and you search desperately for a part that may be vulnerable to an arrow. Your heart pounds and your face is drenched in cold sweat as the Xargath, its jaws agape, swings back its head and lunges straight at you.

If you have the Magnakai Discipline of Animal Control *and* Divination, turn to **186**.
If you do not possess *both* these skills, turn to **12**.

271

You decide to discard your cape and tunic in favour of a suit of leather Drakkarim battle-armour. Disguised as one of these evil warriors, especially with your face hidden behind a black battle-mask, it should be easier to enter Argazad.

Having hidden the bodies and drawn the wagon under cover, you set loose the wagon team and shoo them into the surrounding hills. One of the Drakkarim horses is still close by and you manage to coax it nearer, using some food found in the back of the wagon. While it eats, you tie the reins to a rock to keep it from wandering away, and sift through the crates once more for items that might be of use on the road ahead. You discover the following:

SWORD
AXE
BROADSWORD
BOW
6 ARROWS
QUIVER
DAGGER
MACE
400 KIKA (equivalent to 40 Gold Crowns)

If you decide to keep any of these items remember to make the necessary adjustments to your *Action Chart*.

It is now too dark to continue, so you decide to rest and begin your ride to Argazad at first light. You are now hungry and must eat a Meal or lose 3 ENDURANCE points.

To continue, turn to **200**.

272

The deck is shrouded in smoke but the sound of heavy boots pounding steel plate warns you that a group of Drakkarim marines are approaching, drawn by their comrade's dying screams.

Acting on instinct, you grab the rear of the cannon and revolve it on its mounting until it points directly along the deck. A dozen angry marines emerge from the smoke and their faces freeze in terror when they find themselves staring into the muzzle of their own formidable weapon. 'Death to the Darklords!' you cry, and pull the firing lever.

Turn to **285**.

273

Your senses scream a warning that there is something alive attached to the ceiling of the cabin. It is about to drop on your head.

Pick a number from the *Random Number Table*. If you possess the Magnakai Disciplines of Huntmastery and Pathmanship, add 2 to the number you have picked.

If your total is now *0–4*, turn to **59**.
If it is *5* or more, turn to **23**.

274

You leap from the stern deck and land near the foot of the stairs. Water is pouring into the *Intrepid* at a terrific rate, causing her to list heavily to starboard.

'Abandon ship!' cries Davan, his strong voice carrying above the clangour of striking swords and dying men. As he rushes past you — followed closely by two Kirlundins — he urges you to save yourself before the ship goes down. To stay would be suicidal, and you quickly follow his lead.

Turn to **110**.

275

The golden blade spins through the air and slices deep into the Darklord's shoulder, drawing forth a splash of vile ichor before it clatters noisily to the floor. Kraagenskûl screams in agony, his arm virtually severed from his torso, yet still he manages to touch the silvery liquid. It emits a humming sound, which rises above his cries of pain, and a sparkling mist illuminates the bowl. Swiftly the mist clears to reveal the hideous face of Darklord Gnaag floating upon the surface.

'Aki-amaz narg kog Argazad!' shrieks Kraagenskûl, before you kick the bowl from its plinth, destroying the communicator. The Darklord lashes out with his sword, but you sidestep the wild blow with little difficulty, then stoop to retrieve the Sommerswerd before he strikes a second time.

Darklord Kraagenskûl (wounded):
COMBAT SKILL 36   ENDURANCE 38

This being is immune to Mindblast (but not Psi-surge).

If you win the combat, turn to **318**.

276

Your arrow passes clean through the tendril and shatters against the far wall, drawing a flash of sparks where it punctures it. The harsh, metallic stench of ozone colours the foul air, and the creature withdraws its injured limb. Suddenly, a huge shape explodes from the crevasse, rising at such speed that its features are a blur. It emits a deafening screech and dives towards your chest, lashing you with its injured tendril before you have a chance to draw a hand weapon in your defence. There is another flash and a juddering pain runs the length of your arm, leaving it numb and nerveless: lose 3 ENDURANCE points. Gritting your teeth against the pain, you fumble for a weapon as the creature begins its second swooping attack.

Ictakko (wounded):
COMBAT SKILL 24   ENDURANCE 31

Owing to the speed of its attack, and the wound you have sustained, you are unable to draw a hand weapon until the beginning of the third round of combat. Unless you possess the Magnakai Discipline of Nexus and have reached the Kai rank of Archmaster, you must lose an extra 1 ENDURANCE point every time the Ictakko inflicts a wound during the combat, owing to the numbing effect of its electrical attack.

If you win the combat, turn to **343**.

277

You haul yourself over the rim of the nest and discover the lookout: he is huddled on the floor, shivering with fright. He mutters something but his words are lost in the noise of the destruction raging below. Then the ship rolls violently and you grab the mast to stop yourself from being hurled into the sea. The Xargath has freed its head and is now wreaking havoc amidships, tearing the *Intrepid* asunder with its claws. The massive head rises once more, trailing broken timbers, and lunges for the mast. With an ear-splitting crack it bites it clean in two and, in a flashing instant, you are sent tumbling from your perch to crash upon the debris-strewn deck. Death is instantaneous.

Your life and your mission end here.

278 — *Illustration XVI*

You insert the key and twist it. The lock clicks and the door swings open silently to reveal a stunning sight. A large, low-ceiling room lies beyond, filled with colossal tanks of glass that bubble and seethe with all manner of sorcerous fluids. Glass tubes loop and contort in curious shapes, connecting the tanks and enabling their contents to flow from one to another. The air is heavy with the stench of acids and harsh

XVI. The room is filled with colossal glass tanks and tubes all bubbling with sorcerous fluids chemicals, and the walls are lined from ceiling to floor with stoppered jars, each one filled with a brightly coloured powder, liquid or gas.

On one workbench a curious, arrow-shaped rod is suspended in a field of electrical energy. The crackling fire arcs between two vertical plates of metal, making the arrow glow with a strange phosphorescent light. You take a closer look and see that a lever protruding from the bench itself controls the flow of power. Then you notice that behind the bench there is another door.

If you wish to take a closer look at the rod, turn to **187**.

If you wish to examine the door behind the bench, turn to **54**.

279

Once again your quick wits and instinct for survival have saved you from death. The Giak search party rush forward and surround the boulder where you were spotted, only to find it deserted. In frustration at having let you slip through their fingers, they overturn every rock in the vicinity, cursing and stabbing at anything that moves: they succeed in killing three crabs and a sea-snake! By the time they realize that you have escaped, it is too late for them to catch up; you are over a mile away, running northwards along the beach.

Turn to **157**.

280

Quickly you continue along the tunnel, anxious to put some distance between yourself and the bodies of your foes. You have covered less than a hundred yards when the tunnel splits: one passage slopes gently downwards; the other, steeply upwards.

If you wish to follow the passage downwards, turn to **116**.

If you decide to climb the passage sloping upwards, turn to **316**.

281

Your stern commands seem to impress this Giak soldier. Humbly, he bows his head and beckons you to follow him as he climbs back through the trapdoor and down a stair that descends into the heart of the building. There, stacked on countless shelves, are row upon row of coiled steel cables, girders, iron bolts, and myriad other parts destined for the fleet of ironclads at anchor in Argazad harbour.

You follow the bow-legged Giak out of the building and through a maze of garbage-choked streets, past rusting tenements and squalid huts, to an iron tower at the centre of the city. Unlike everywhere else, this tower appears to have escaped the effects of the corrosive atmosphere: its surfaces are dull yet free from any sign of decay. The Giak speaks with another who guards its open entrance and immediately he stands aside, allowing you to enter the tower's gloomy ground floor.

Turn to **346**.

282

'You wield a weapon imbued with great power, Lone Wolf,' says Rimoah, glancing at the Sommerswerd sheathed at your side. 'Be sure to use it well. Now that you possess the wisdom of the Lorestones, you will discover new strengths within its golden blade. It is the bane of the Darklords — the instrument of their destruction. Yet by the very nature of its power it can alert them to your presence and betray your identity.'

He reaches to his waist and unbuckles a seemingly plain leather swordbelt and scabbard. 'I have prepared this scabbard from materials impregnated with korlinium. It will contain and keep hidden the powers of the Sommerswerd,' he says, handing you the accoutrements. 'Remember, to unsheathe the Sommerswerd inside the Darklands is to light a beacon of warning that Gnaag and his fell minions will surely see. Only when you have Gnaag within striking distance should you draw your blade to seal his doom.'

You discard your old scabbard in favour of Rimoah's and take heed of his advice. (Mark the Korlinium Scabbard as a Special Item on your *Action Chart*. You need not discard another item in its favour if you already carry the maximum number of Special Items allowed.)

Turn to **229**.

283

From the flickering scarlet doorway of a tower to your right comes a line of robed figures, every one of them dressed in red. They are led by a squat, horny-skinned creature with baleful, milky-coloured eyes. These eyes roll like balls of mist inside its head as the creature emits a fiendish howl, and points at you with its clawed hand.

If you wish to confront this creature and its followers, turn to **104**.

If you wish to try to evade these creatures, turn to **242**.

284

Patiently you wait until the Drakkarim and Giaks are snoring soundly, then you leave your hiding place and slip away undetected. Your plan is to ambush the Drakkar who was caught cheating, at dawn when he rides back to Argazad alone. By discarding your cape and tunic in favour of his battle-armour it should be far easier to enter the naval base unnoticed, especially on horseback and with your face obscured by one of the grotesque battle-masks that all Drakkarim wear.

Three miles along the trail you find the ideal place to launch your ambush, where the stony track passes between a cluster of huge rocks. There you lie in wait for the dawn and with it the arrival of your victim. While you wait, you must eat a Meal or lose 3 ENDURANCE points.

To continue, turn to **146**.

285

There is a loud bang and a wave of heat rolls over you as the cannon spits its deadly missile at the advancing Drakkarim. It bores through their ranks and slams into the wheelhouse with shuddering force. Jets of yellow flame roar from a jagged hole, illuminating the grim remains of what a moment before were enemy marines. Then the deck jumps up and slaps the soles of your feet. The missile has penetrated the ironclad's magazine, and, in an instant, the vessel is blown apart. The last thing you remember before darkness obliterates your senses is an eye-searing flash of white and scarlet fire.

Turn to **125**.

286

As you watch the Vassagonians leave, you edge nearer to Kraagenskûl and prepare yourself to launch a surprise attack. You will need all your speed and skill if you are to catch him off-guard. From the bottom of the stairs you hear the steel door click shut and immediately you spin around to face your enemy. But he has a plan of his own and it is he who catches you by surprise. A crackling arc of blue electrical fire surges from his hand and connects with your chest, shaking you like a helpless puppet on the tip of a fiery lance.

'Now tell me everything you know!' he growls, as he increases the current. It is a torture that he has employed countless times, and always it has elicited the truth from his human victims.

Your skin tingles and the charge causes you to shiver, yet you feel no pain. Staring down, you see that the crackling bolt is being drawn to the Golden Amulet that hangs around your chest: its magical properties are neutralizing the evil charge. Kraagenskûl senses that something is wrong. He breaks off his attack, his bulbous eyes filled with fearful suspicion. He steps back, then utters a curse in the dark tongue, which echoes like thunder around the walls. Black mist pours from his fingers, swirling into a cone that grows in his bony palm. Shadow shapes writhe at the core, then gush towards you, engulfing you in a choking flood of deadly Crypt Spawn.

If you possess the Sommerswerd and wish to use it, turn to **57**.

If you possess the Dagger of Vashna and wish to use it, turn to **171**.

If you possess neither of these Special Items, or choose not to use either of them, turn to **109**.

287

Your arrow flies straight and true, hitting the creature squarely in the head and killing him instantly. The cries of your pursuers are growing louder, so you shoulder your bow quickly beneath your robe and run towards the entrance to the tower.

Turn to **308**.

288

Part of the heavy boom glances off your shoulder, making you lose your balance and fall to your knees: lose 2 ENDURANCE points. The wound causes you to react sluggishly to the burning canvas now draped over your body and, in a matter of seconds, the flames and smoke completely engulf you. Instinctively, you fight to free yourself, then suddenly you realize that your clothes are unaffected by the blaze, and that the tongues of fire that are licking your hands and face cause you no pain whatsoever. Without haste or urgency you cast aside the blazing sailcloth and emerge unburned.

Turn to **101**.

289

You are in combat with a wounded Vladoka – an elite Nadziranim temple guard. Despite his injury, you cannot evade his attacks and must fight him to the death.

Vladoka (wounded):
COMBAT SKILL 22   ENDURANCE 25

Owing to the power of the weapon he wields, this denizen of Helgedad is immune to Mindblast and Psi-surge.

If you win the combat, turn to **308**.

290

The Sergeant crashes lifelessly to the deck and, for a few moments, the troops that were fighting by his side stare down at his body in shocked disbelief. For six years he had led them to glory – his battle-skills and cunning ensuring their survival – and now he lies dead, killed by a Sommlending. Taking advantage of their stunned state, you cleave a path up the staircase and force your way towards the helm. You are within ten feet of the ship's wheel when Davan screams a warning: 'Archer above you!'

You glance up into the rigging and a cold spike of fear stabs your heart when you glimpse the gloating face of a Drakkar marine. With one hand he holds a bow and with the other he draws back an arrow to his chin. He mouths a curse and lets fly the deadly shaft.

Pick a number from the *Random Number Table*. If you have the Magnakai Discipline of Huntmastery add 2 to the number you have picked. If you have completed the Lore-circle of the Spirit, add 3 to the number.

If your total is now *0–3*, turn to **122**.
If it is *4–7*, turn to **53**.
If it is *8* or more, turn to **321**.

291

'Gaz dik!' roars the guard, and reaches for his wide-bladed battle sword. Using his psychic probe – the crystal box-like device that he removed from his pouch – he has detected that it is your intention to destroy the Transfusor and kill Darklord Gnaag. Instantly, the two guards spring into action, forcing you to retreat along the corridor as you fumble to unsheathe a weapon.

Imperial Sector Guards:
COMBAT SKILL 30   ENDURANCE 38

These guards are immune to Mindblast (but not Psi-surge).

If you possess the Sommerswerd, and wish to unsheathe it, turn to **208**.
If you win and the combat lasts five rounds or less, turn to **95**.

(continued over)

If you win and the combat last longer than five
rounds, turn to **199**.

292

The speed and ferocity of your attack take the Drakkarim gunners by surprise. Frantically they fumble to
draw their short swords as you leap amongst them and
strike your first blows.

Drakkarim Gunners:
COMBAT SKILL 21   ENDURANCE 30

Owing to the speed of your attack, ignore any
ENDURANCE point losses you may sustain in the first
two rounds of combat.

If you win the combat, turn to **272**.

293

'Be on your guard at all times,' he says, solemnly. 'The
lesser creatures of Helgedad are a ruthlessly
treacherous breed, forever preoccupied with their
complex political intrigues. You will need to be doubly
cunning if you are not to fall foul of their wilful
machinations. The robe you wear marks you as one
of Darklord Ghanesh's minions. He is far away at
present, leading his horde in distant Lencia, but his
absence will be of little help to you. Avoid all who wear
robes of green and scarlet, for they are followers of
Xog and Taktaal, Ghanesh's closest rivals. But above
all, avoid those who wear silver-grey, the same colour
as yourself, for they know their own kind and are sure
to see through your disguise.'

He walks across the chamber and picks up a curious-
looking device by which he is able to tell the time of

day. 'Come, follow me. Now you will learn how you are to breach the defences of Helgedad.'

Turn to **260**.

294

The Kirlundin close the gaps and the Drakkarim are soon repulsed, enabling your command to catch their breath and retrieve their wounded. Yet the lull in the fighting is but a brief respite before the enemy surge forward once more, this time with even greater fury and determination. The crash and screech of combat is carried on an ever rising wind that causes the linked vessels to roll and pitch violently.

If you possess the Magnakai Discipline of Divination, turn to **89**.

If you do not possess this skill, turn to **172**.

295 – *Illustration XVII*

The harbour and neighbouring wharfs are filled with noise and furious industry. An army of slaves and Drakkarim overseers are at work servicing the ironclad fleet, their lanterns flickering along the rows of shiny black decks as they toil to maintain the vessels in fighting trim.

As you enter the harbour square, you pass a line of wagons laden with heavy machinery, which are queuing to enter a dry dock. There, illuminated by the glare of huge oil lamps, is the largest ship you have ever seen – a monstrous ironclad juggernaut bristling with awesome weaponry. You stop to stare at this terrifying vessel, and overhear two Drakkarim engineers talking about their work. Your blood runs cold when

XVII. Inside the harbour square you stop and stare at a
monstrous ironclad juggernaut

you hear one of them reveal why this juggernaut is being built. It is to be used to destroy Holmgard, your country's capital city.

> If you wish to enter the dry dock and attempt to sabotage the juggernaut, turn to **76**.
> If you decide to ride on and continue your search for some means of transportation to Aarnak, turn to **97**.

296

Less than a mile along the rock shore, you catch sight of something moving in the shadows. You use your advanced Kai skill to magnify your vision and are able to see a patrol of Giaks, searching the water's edge for survivors of the battle. Some they help, carrying them on stretchers to their encampment perched high on a overhanging cliff; others, presumably crew from the Intrepid, they stab repeatedly with their spears and leave for the sharks to claim. Forewarned by your skill, you begin to paddle away from the patrol, keen to avoid their chilling welcome.

Turn to **174**.

297

Having satisfied yourself that you have overlooked no items of use, you decide to make your way to the heart of Aarnak. Your trek takes you into a maze of garbage-choked streets lined with rusting tenements and squalid huts. Hordes of slaves move to and fro, their backs bent by years of heavy labour. As you turn a corner you are confronted by a procession of these sad creatures, led by a squad of Giaks.

The leader, a squat Giak sergeant wearing a doom-wolf pelt, commands you to halt. Drakkarim are rare visitors to Aarnak, the human constitution being ill-suited to the hostile atmosphere, so the sight of you walking unescorted through the city streets, clad in Drakkarim armour, stirs his deepest suspicions. You continue walking, and immediately he raises his clawed hand – it is a signal to his squad to advance and surround you. You turn to run, but when you see that all the Giak soldiers are armed with bows, discretion prompts you to try a different tactic. Boldly you demand that the sergeant take you to the Slavemaster and, to your relief, he agrees.

The sergeant, and a handful of his troops, take you towards the centre of the city, to a solitary tower standing in the middle of an open square. It is a curious building, tall and unbent, its surface free from any sign of decay. The sergeant speaks with another who guards its open entrance and immediately he stands aside, allowing you to enter the tower's gloomy ground floor.

Turn to **346**.

Your Kai skill enables you to detect that the creature outside your cabin door possesses magical abilities. You also sense that he, or she, is not emitting an aura of hostility.

If you wish to open your cabin door, turn to **85**.
If you decide to ignore the knock, turn to **144**.

299

You strike your killing blow, laying open the great beast's throat. It rears up, shuddering, its green eyes rolling wildly in their sockets. Then it gives vent to a hideous, gurgling scream that grows louder until, with a mighty splash, the Xargath topples backwards into the fog-wreathed sea.

Turn to **217**.

300

Dawn arrives, its hazy light barely brightening the banks of grey cloud that swirl above this bleak and desolate land. The rain has ceased but the cold wind still blows strongly, bringing patches of frost that whiten the stony soil. You check your equipment and take stock of your provisions before setting off towards a distant line of hills. You are aware that the dawn light has increased the chances of your being found by a Giak patrol should you stay too long in any one place, especially so near to the shore.

It is nearly noon when finally you reach the top of the ridge and stare down at the valley that lies beyond. It is a barren landscape of endless pits and crags, jagged boulders and scree. A rough, foot-worn track follows a stream that winds its way back to its source, deep among a towering range of mountains that dominates the horizon. Using your map and your Kai tracking and hunting skills, you conclude that the mountains are the north-western tip of the Durncrag Range. Beyond them must lie the Gulf of Helenag and the Darklord naval base of Argazad. A feeling of dread overwhelms you as you realize that more than 300 miles of hostile terrain lie between you and Aarnak, the stronghold where you are to rendezvous with the Slavemaster. Silently you stare at the forbidding mountains and rack your brains for a solution to your predicament. At length, you formulate a new plan of action.

Turn to **196**.

301

As you scour the city below, you spot two possible landing sites. One is an open patch of ground near an iron foundry; the other is the flat roof of a building situated on the bank of the estuary.

If you wish to land near the foundry, turn to **162**.
If you decide to land the Zlanbeast on the roof of the building, turn to **221**.

302

You draw the seed from your pocket and hurl it down into the darkness. It strikes steel and explodes with a blinding flash, illuminating for an instant the cramped control cabin and the startled faces of the Drakkarim crew. You see that they outnumber you many times over, but at least the flash buys you precious seconds in which to make your escape to the deck above.

Turn to **169**.

303

Further along the tunnel lies a cavern, empty save for a mass of squeaking bats hanging from the stalactites in the roof. At your approach they begin to panic. They swarm and encircle the rough-hewn walls before diving into a dark crevasse that splits the floor in two. The only exit, other than the tunnel by which you entered, is a passage on the far side of the crevasse. Foul air rises from the dark abyss, laden with a heavy odour that reminds you of maggoty meat.

If you have completed the Lore-circle of the Spirit *and* the Lore-circle of Solaris, turn to **315**.

If you wish to approach the crevasse and look for a way to get across, turn to **44**.

If you decide to abandon the chamber and attempt to retrace your route back to the Giak outpost, turn to **206**.

304

You squeeze into a space between the rocks and listen to the grind of the wagon's wheels on the rough stone trail as it draws steadily nearer. Then a Drakkar voice cries out: 'Koga! Okim dag nadulheza!' The sound stops abruptly. You strain your ears for an indication of what the enemy are doing, but all you can hear are muffled voices and the jingle of bridles and bits. Then you hear the Drakkarim escorts leave the trail and dismount close to where you are hiding. Your pulse quickens as you realize that they are preparing to strike camp here overnight.

Fortunately, because they are deep inside their own territory, the Drakkarim do not bother to inspect their surroundings and your presence goes undetected. You listen intently to their conversations but discover little useful information except that they are from Argazad and are on their way to the outpost at the mouth of the Durncrag Pass. After eating, they settle down to a session of gambling. They have been playing for only a few minutes when one of the Drakkarim is accused of cheating. A violent argument breaks out and bloodshed is averted only when their commander, a sergeant, steps in to break it up. He finds a fistful of cards wedged up the accused Drakkar's sleeve. Angrily, he denounces the cheat and orders him to return to Argazad at first light. The game is brought to a close, and, as the disgruntled Drakkarim get ready to sleep, a bold plan springs into your mind that could make your journey through the Darklands and your entry into Argazad much easier.

Turn to **284**.

305

The still water is set to boiling by the shoal of glistening fish, as they swarm around the *Intrepid*. They have been drawn here by the warmth of the ship's hull, and as you stare down into the seething turmoil, you estimate that there must be hundreds of thousands of fish directly beneath the keel. You watch with fascination until you recall something about the sea carp that you learned when you were a novice at the Kai monastery, something that sends a tingle of premonition down your spine.

The tales and legends of the northern seas tell of the Xargath, a fearsome breed of giant reptilian sea creature that inhabits the black depths of the Kaltesee. Once, a century ago, the fishermen of Sommerlund trawled these waters and grew rich on the fruits of their labours, for the sea carp were plentiful and the markets of Sommerlund and Durenor paid highly for their catch. Trade thrived until the Xargath appeared and began to attack their boats. So devastating were the attacks, and so terrifying were the descriptions of the Xargath by those fortunate few who survived them, that all fishing in these waters was abandoned and has never been resumed.

A swarm of sea carp, as huge as that which now surrounds the *Intrepid*, is sure to attract a hungry Xargath. You turn to look for the captain, to warn him of the danger his ship is in, when suddenly the shoal cease their thrashing and fall silent and still.

Turn to **60**.

306

As you strike the blow that seals the creature's doom, it disappears, leaving no trace whatsoever. Gnaag roars his anger and lopes awkwardly towards the Transfusor, desperate to recall his fellow Darklords to the Black City. You block his path and feel an eerie force — a tingling electric coldness — pass between you. With an unholy scream, Darklord Gnaag unsheathes his sword, Nadazgada, and prepares to engage you in a battle that will determine the destiny of Magnamund.

If you possess the Sommerswerd, turn to **214**.

If you possess the Dagger of Vashna *or* Helshezag (the sword of Darklord Kraagenskûl), and wish to use either of them, turn to **88**.

If you possess none of these Special Items, turn to **3**.

307

The fatique of your ordeal is dulling your senses and making it increasingly difficult to keep your eyes open, so, using your backpack for a pillow, you settle down and slip readily into a deep sleep. However, it seems as though you have only just closed your eyes when a strange snickering sound stirs you to wakefulness.

Crouching at the entrance to the cave, and silhouetted by the flashes of storm lightning, is a hulking creature with yellow, cat-like eyes. It emits a hungry growl and leaps at your prone body, hoping to crush you beneath its huge bulk. But your reflexes thwart its aim — you roll aside and jump to your feet as it hits the ground, which shudders beneath the vast stone weight. Quickly the creature recovers and leaps once more, its hairy, lipless mouth opening in anticipation.

Egorgh: COMBAT SKILL 25　ENDURANCE 34

Owing to the speed of its attack you are unable to make use of a bow. This creature is particularly susceptible to psychic attack; double all bonuses you would normally receive if using Mindblast or Psi-surge during the combat.

If you win the combat, turn to **153**.

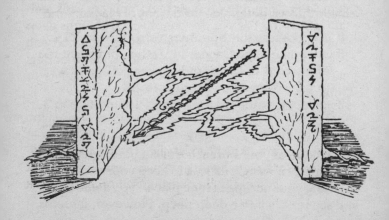

308

You stoop over the body of the dead guard and search quickly through the pockets of his robe. They contain two items: a Black Key and a Black Cube.

If you possess the Magnakai Discipline of Divination, turn to **179**.

If you do not possess this skill, you may take either or both of the Backpack Items, or leave them undisturbed, turn to **263**.

309

You spin the ship's wheel to starboard and pray for the wind to fill her sails and carry her clear of the first enemy vessel. Anxiously, you glance at the second ironclad steaming directly towards the stern with unnerving speed, its deck crammed with more troops poised to leap aboard. At first, the *Intrepid* responds to the rudder and you feel her swing about. But the escape is short-lived: the Drakkarim have secured her with hooks and ropes and she cannot break free.

With a shuddering crash, the ironclad rams the side, knocking everyone off their feet. You are sent reeling across the deck as the enemy craft ploughs deep into the hull, demolishing the steerage and carrying away a large section of the stern. Icy water thunders into the hold and immediately the ship begins to founder.

'Darg ash ruzzar!' bellow the enemy as they climb towards the deck, jostling and bullying each other in their eagerness to begin the battle. Their leader, a bull-necked brute armed with dirk and scimitar, is the first to appear at the rail. He pulls himself on to the deck and comes rushing forward, his eyes wide with blood-frenzy as he prepares to strike you down.

If you have a bow and wish to use it, turn to **77**.

If you possess the Sommerswerd and wish to use it, turn to **128**.

If you choose to draw a hand weapon and ready yourself to receive his attack, turn to **213**.

310

The Death Knight, silhouetted by the glow of the harbour lights, presents you with an easy target. Silently, you draw an arrow to your lips and send it burrowing deep between the plates of black steel that protect his spine. He stiffens, then collapses in a heap by the parapet wall. A quick search of his body uncovers the following items:

> SPEAR
> AXE
> DAGGER
> 60 KIKA (equivalent to 6 Gold Crowns)
> BOTTLE OF WINE
> POUCH OF TOBACCO
> PIPE
> IRON KEY
> ENOUGH FOOD FOR 1 MEAL

If you wish to keep any of the above items, remember to record them on your *Action Chart*.

To continue, turn to **257**.

311

Three times you struck a blow and three times a Giak heart beat its last. Now, without pausing even to catch your breath, you take off along the trail and begin the steep climb towards the cliff top. Angry shouts and curses echo in your wake, alerting another party of Giaks on the cliffs above to your presence. They race to the end of the trail and await your appearance, determined to catch you and then kill you at their leisure. You sense the danger and leave the steep trail at the first opportunity. You wait for your pursuers to pass, then double back to the beach. By the time the Giaks realize that you are no longer climbing the trail, it is too late for them to catch up; you are on the beach, more than a mile away to the north.

Turn to **157**.

312

Still shaking from the shock of this encounter, you examine the ghastly creature carefully, using the tip of your weapon to lift back its many folds of rubbery grey flesh. It is equipped with two sets of snake-like fangs, both of which ooze a sticky yellow fluid. Your senses tell you that this fluid is a deadly venom, capable of killing a victim in a matter of seconds. Whoever placed this Plaak in your cabin was attempting to assassinate you.

You flick the remains of the creature under your bunk. As you rise to your feet, you hear a loud, intermittent whistle sounding on the deck above: it is the signal that Helgedad has been sighted by the lookout. With your heart pounding at the thought of seeing the Darklord's most infamous stronghold for the first time, you leave your cabin and ascend to the level above.

Turn to **326**.

313

Your arrow strikes the creature's ear but it fails to penetrate the ear canal. Instead it is spun away by a ridge of horny scales and arcs harmlessly into the sea. Cursing your misfortune, you reach for a hand weapon as the Xargath advances unceasingly, its jaws widening as it prepares to swallow you whole.

Turn to **344**.

314

The Death Knight sergeant has a reputation for cruelty that is matched only by his wanton greed. He is used to total obedience from his troops, and when you fail to answer his command he becomes suspicious. Arrogantly, he swaggers towards you and repeats his command, his hand reaching casually for a barbed whip which he carries holstered on his hip. It is too late to attempt an escape, but the fear of what may happen serves to sharpen your survival instincts. As you stare into his cruel eyes, you sense that all is not lost: he may let you pass if you offer him a large bribe.

If you possess some Kika and wish to offer them as a bribe, turn to **202**.

If you possess some Gold Crowns and wish to offer them as a bribe, turn to **126**.

If you possess a Medal and wish to offer that as a bribe, turn to **269**.

315

Your highly developed senses detect that something is rising from the depths of the crevasse, something huge, hungry and hostile.

If you have a bow and wish to take aim at the crevasse, turn to **103**.

If you wish to unsheathe a hand weapon and get ready to defend yourself, turn to **226**.

If you decide to escape from the cavern while you can, turn to **206**.

316

The passage services a staircase that ascends to the surface. You climb the stairs and emerge in a gloomy square flanked by four tall towers.

If you possess the Magnakai Discipline of Divination, and have reached the rank of Archmaster, turn to **124**.

If you do not possess this skill, or have yet to attain this level of Kai training, turn to **283**.

317

Quickly you search the bodies of the Drakkarim. You discover the following items which could be of use to you during your mission:

     3 SWORDS (Weapons)
     2 AXES (Weapons)
     2 DAGGERS (Weapons)
     1 BOW (Weapons)
     4 ARROWS (Weapons list)
     1 ROPE (Backpack Items)
     1 POUCH OF HERBS (Backpack Items)

While searching the officer's body, you discover that he is wearing a vest of chainmail beneath his leather battle-jacket. It is forged from links of a strange, blue-black metal that gives off a strong aura of magic.

If you wish to take this magical chainmail vest, turn to **63**.

If you choose not to take the vest, turn to **188**.

318

The instant you strike the killing blow, Kraagenskûl emits a howl so loud that it shakes the very foundations of the building, a howl that conveys his total despair and eternal damnation. He falls, yet as he does so, his withered frame vanishes before your eyes. A tattered grey robe and a flickering black sword are all that mark the place where his doom was sealed.

Quickly you leave the chamber by a stair that leads to the roof. The Zlanbeast, Kraagenskûl's personal winged mount, sniffs the air and shuffles along its perch with a nervous, rolling gait. It senses that you are its natural enemy and it is determined to resist your attempts to subdue it. More than an hour elapses before you have control over the creature, and can climb into the saddle without it trying frantically to hook and gouge you with its great curved claws. You pull on the reins and urge the beast skywards, eager to leave this port of evil, but no sooner has it cleared the roof than you are engulfed by a squadron of screeching Kraan swooping down from the night sky. They have flown all the way from Kaag, a Darkland fortress to the south, after being alerted to your presence here by Darklord Gnaag. Valiantly you fight to defend your life, but the odds are overwhelmingly against you. The Kraan drag you from your saddle and you meet your doom upon the hard, unyielding cobblestones of Argazad harbour.

Your life and your mission end here.

319

Your sharp Kai reflexes save you from the spinning blade. It arcs over your head and scrapes the side of the cannon, drawing a line of sparks along the barrel before splashing harmlessly into the sea.

Acting on instinct, you grab the rear of the cannon and swing it around to face the onrushing Drakkarim marines. Their faces freeze in terror when they find themselves staring into the muzzle of their own formidable, doom-dealing machine. 'Death to the Darklords!' you cry, and pull the firing lever.

Turn to **285**.

320 – *Illustration XVIII (overleaf)*

You walk through the armoury, and past an arsenal of fiendish devices that have yet to be unleashed on the allied armies of the freelands, but are destined soon to be shipped to the battle front to speed Gnaag's conquest of Magnamund. A passage at the far end of the hall takes you past a barracks-like room where Naziranim sorcerers are busily engaged in the testing of new psychic weapons upon a group of grey-skinned slaves, mindless Grolth from the swamps of the Tadatizaga. Their pitiful screams of agony make your blood run cold, yet you dare not intervene to prevent their torture for fear of jeopardizing your mission. Hurriedly you climb a staircase that emerges at the foot of a monstrous tower, as black as death itself. Two fireballs split open the rolling black clouds and in the brilliance of their explosions you see a huge metallic flag flying from the tower's crystal spire. It is

XVIII. You have found what you have been looking for:
The Tower of the Damned

emblazoned with the emblem of Darklord Gnaag, and at once you know that you have found what you are looking for: the Tower of the Damned.

As your eyes move down the tower, you notice a large oval platform jutting out from the black steel wall. Perched on this platform is an Imperial Zlanbeast, similar to the one that bore you to Aarnak. It, too, bears Gnaag's sign, branded deep in its leathery hide. Its presence suggests that its master is in residence, and as you cross the courtyard and walk towards the tower door, your senses tingle in anticipation of the confrontation that awaits you within.

As you climb the steps that lead to the door, it slides open to reveal the outline of a guard silhouetted against a background of scarlet fire. In a claw-tipped hand he holds several slivers of crystal, each a different colour, and, as you reach the top of the steps, he draws a silvery-grey one and points it at your face. 'State your name, minion of Ghanesh!' he commands, 'or begone from the Tower of the Damned.'

You sense that the guard does not suspect you of being an imposter, he is merely performing a routine check on all who visit the tower. To have come this far into the Imperial Sector means that you have passed through several checkpoints already, and so the guard does not regard you as a threat to his master's safety. In order to be allowed to pass, you must state the name of the Liganim whose identity and robe you are using as a disguise.

If you wish to say your name is Cagath, turn to **138**.
If you wish to say your name is Morgath, turn to **19**.

321

You twist aside and the arrow thuds harmlessly into the deck. The archer bares his teeth as he reaches for another arrow, but before he can fire again, his aim is spoiled by two of his comrades, who rush forward to hack at you with axe and sword. Davan protects your back, holding off the marines who are attempting to climb the stairs. You evade the first blows of your enemies, side-stepping a lunge and ducking a wild swipe, then strike back with deadly speed and unerring accuracy. Both scream and fall simultaneously, dying with a look of surprise fixed on their cruel faces.

Turn to **209**.

322

The creatures on the ramp, whom the Giaks were overseeing, pay no attention whatsoever to the deaths of their guards. Mechanically they continue their toil as if incapable of any other function. Quickly you check the bodies for anything of use, and discover the following items:

> 3 SWORDS
> DAGGER
> PIPE
> 40 KIKA (equivalent to 4 Gold Crowns)
> WHIP (Backpack Item)

If you decide to keep any of these items, remember to amend your *Action Chart* accordingly.

Turn to **297**.

323

As you stare at the ruins, a strange feeling of unease engulfs your body; at the same time a nervous energy makes your skin tingle and fills your mind with disturbing images. Your highly developed mind skills are sensitive to the psychic residues of events that took place here two thousand years ago.

This land once belonged to a colony of creatures called the Nebora, a sentient race of winged men who evolved during the Golden Age of the Shianti. The city of Neboran, the core of their civilization, was located here on what was once a rich and fertile coastal plain. The demise of the Shianti heralded the rise of the Darklords in Northern Magnamund, and the beginning of the War of Desecration in which the Nebora, and many other races, were exterminated. This ruined tower is all that remains of the wondrous city of Neboran where, in the year MS3250, the entire Nebora race were trapped and slaughtered by the Darklords of Helgedad.

Turn to **191**.

324

Quickly you draw an arrow from your quiver and set its notch to your bow string. The light of the fireball explosion has long since faded and in the gloom you find it difficult to pinpoint your target with great accuracy.

Pick a number from the *Random Number Table* and add any weapon skill bonuses to which you are entitled. If you possess the Magnakai Discipline of

Huntmastery, and have reached the Kai rank of Archmaster, add an additional 3 points to your total.

If your total is now *0–4*, turn to **25**.
If it is *5–9*, turn to **193**.
If it is *10* or more, turn to **287**.

325

The night wind is blowing in your favour and Captain Borse is keen to put to sea without delay. He has ordered the crew to run up every foot of canvas the masts of the *Intrepid* will bear, so that she will approach the Darklord warships that blockade the coast at full speed. With luck, she will slip through their line before they have a chance to close formation. It is a bold plan, but the captain and his crew have run the blockade more than a dozen times in the past year and they are confident that tonight they will also be successful.

Guided by the stars and the distant glimmer of the moonlit shore, the *Intrepid* makes rapid headway through the waters of the Toran Gulf. As it nears the open sea, you decide to offer your services as a lookout and go in search of Captain Borse. You find him on the forecastle deck with a group of keen-eyed Kirlundin marines, who are scanning the blackness for some sign of the enemy.

If you have the Magnakai Discipline of Huntmastery, and have reached the rank of Archmaster, turn to **47**.

If you do not possess this skill, or have yet to reach this level of Kai training, turn to **256**.

326

With trepidation, you peer through the thick and grimy glass of a hull porthole and gaze upon the awesome spectacle that is Helgedad. Perched upon an isle of granite at the centre of a vast, fiery chasm stands the mighty city-fortress, the very core of a cancer that threatens to infect and destroy all that is good in Magnamund. Great walls of black steel encircle it, giving rise to a thousand spiky towers and turrets which harbour the masters and the minions of darkness. Above the city hovers a seething pall of black smoke that keeps it forever in shadow. Fed by the fumes from the volcanic craters of the Naogizaga, this cloud is made all the more noisome by the foul discharges of the Nadziranim laboratories, the weapon furnaces, and the hellish breeding pits at the base of the chasm.

Irregularly the darkness is lit by fireballs that seem to form spontaneously among the black vapours. They spin and soar above the city like demonic meteors, before exploding or simply melting away in a rain of sparks. A bridge of twisted black steel joins Helgedad to the wastelands beyond, and as the Lajakeka slowly grinds its way across this span, you look down into the fiery depths of the Nengud-kor-Adez, the Lake of Blood, and your courage quails at the terrible sight that meets your gaze.

Turn to **150**.

327

The tide is carrying you towards a long, grey cliff line, made ominous by the flickering glow of burning battle debris. A flock of ugly black birds circle overhead. They dive repeatedly to retrieve carrion, then soar away to their nests in the clifff wall. Two of the evil-looking creatures swoop down on you, mistaking your still form for a ready feast, and attempt to tear the skin from your face with their razor-sharp beaks.

If you possess the Magnakai Discipline of Animal Control, and have reached the Kai rank of Primate or more, turn to **207**.

If you do not possess this skill, or have yet to reach this level of Kai training, you can attempt to defend yourself with a bow: turn to **49**.

Or you can fend them off with a hand weapon: turn to **337**.

328

You follow a cobblestoned alleyway and soon arrive at a large square, flanked to the north, south and west by warehouses, yet dominated by a smaller building on the east side. Its granite walls are festooned with black flags bearing the emblem of a silver ship and fiery sword, and atop its flat roof there sits a huge, winged creature with mottled grey skin — an Imperial Zlanbeast. You watch with grim fascination as the beast feeds from a pile of horse carcasses stacked beside its perch. Then a daring thought comes to mind. If you could reach the roof of the building and steal the Zlanbeast, it would be possible to reach Aarnak by air in a matter of hours, rather than the days it would take by land or sea.

After riding once around the building to assess its defences, you leave your horse tethered to a rail near **a side entrance and approach the only door that** appears to be unguarded. It is locked, but the crude drawbolt that secures it proves no match for your basic Kai skill of mind over matter. The bolt clicks back, the door swings open, and you enter the building unseen.

Turn to **140**.

329

Drawing on your considerable psychic powers, you raise a shield to deflect the energies that are assaulting your mind. Taktaal shrieks with anger and surprise as he senses that you are not what you appear to be. He has seen through your disguise and your true identity shocks him to the core.

Turn to **176**.

330

For the following two days and nights the *Intrepid* remains a prisoner of the windless fog. Davan and his crewmen work tirelessly to repair the ship, and come the morning of the third day, when a gentle breeze arises with the dawn, the main mast is secure and the sails are patched and ready to carry the ship onward. With the port side still holed and storms a constant threat in the open reaches of the Kaltesee, it has been decided that the safest course to steer is towards the coast. Then, should a sudden squall threaten, or a gale arise, the ship could run to shelter in one of the hundreds of coves that indent the rugged shore east of Point Vashna. However, to sail along this stretch of coastline is to risk hazards that could prove as dangerous as any storm. Darkland ironclads, unstable in high seas, favour the coast when venturing to and from their base at Argazad, and the cliffs and shores themselves are peppered with watchtowers and Giak encampments.

By early afternoon the fog has cleared and the *Intrepid* is making good headway through the cold, sparkling waves. League after glittering league fall away to the stern until, an hour or two before sunset, the lookout catches sight of the coast. 'Land ahoy!' he calls. 'Land afore the bow!' The crew are cheered by the news, feeling safer now that they are within sight of land, but their spirits are soon dampened when the lookout calls out again, this time in alarm. 'Enemy off the starboard bow!'

Turn to **100**.

331

Without the magical protection afforded you by the Golden Amulet, you soon succumb to the hellish temperatures and poisonous atmosphere of Helgedad. As your skin begins to blister and your lungs become paralysed, you fight desperately to hold on to life, but it is a fight you cannot hope to win.

Tragically, your life and your mission end here, beneath the streets of Helgedad.

332

Your lightning reactions save you from being hit by the heavy boom but you cannot avoid the burning canvas. In a matter of seconds you are completely engulfed in an envelope of fire and smoke. Instinctively, you fight to free yourself, then suddenly you realize that your clothes are unaffected by the blaze, and that the tongues of fire licking your hands and face cause you no pain whatsoever. Without haste or urgency you cast aside the blazing sailcloth and emerge completely unscathed.

Turn to **101**.

333

The winged reptilian tries its best to prevent you from climbing on to its back. It lunges with its beak and you suffer several painful wounds before finally managing to subdue it to your will: lose 4 ENDURANCE points.

Once the creature accepts you as its new master, it becomes totally obedient to your commands. You settle back in the comfortable saddle, then pull on the great gem-encrusted reins and urge it skywards. The roof of Kraagenskûl's headquarters, and then Argazad itself, fall away at a breathtaking speed as the creature climbs into the night sky. High above the ironclad fleet, you turn the Zlanbeast towards the west and begin your flight to Aarnak.

Turn to **36**.

334

A great cloud of dust and debris billows from the gaping hole, and as it slowly begins to clear, you see that most of the enemy warriors have been swallowed up by the collapsing deck. Beyond the hole you glimpse Davan, with a handful of the crew, defending the stern deck against an attacking swarm of Drakkarim, who outnumber them by at least two to one. Then you realize the enemy plan: if they can capture the helm they will be able to steer the *Intrepid* towards the coast and beach her in the shallows.

Quickly you climb into the rigging and swing across to the stern deck by means of a trailing rope. Davan sees you and gives a cheer as you jump from the rope and land among the enemy. You unsheathe your weapon and begin cleaving a path towards your beleaguered allies, who shout encouragement as you draw nearer. 'For Sommerlund!' you cry, and they take up your battle call. Then Davan's voice rings above the noise of battle: it is a cry of warning —

'Archer above you!'

You glance upwards and a cold spike of fear stabs your heart. Staring down at you is the gloating face of a Drakkar. He holds a bow in his hands, and prepares to fire an arrow at your head. He mouths a curse, then lets fly his deadly shaft.

Pick a number from the *Random Number Table*. If **you have the Magnakai Discipline of Huntmastery,** add 2 to the number you have picked. If you have completed the Lore-circle of the Spirit, add 3 to the number.

If your total is now *0–3*, turn to **122**.
If it is *4–7*, turn to **53**.
If it is *8* or more, turn to **321**.

335

The Giak groans and clutches at his wounds as he staggers backwards and crashes down upon the barrels and cases. Curious to discover what they are transporting, you roll his body aside, prise open the largest crate, and rummage through the contents. It is filled with Giak and Drakkarim uniforms, enough to dress a hundred troops. The other cases contain an assortment of weapons and other military equipment, and the barrels are full of a wine too foul to even think of tasting. Then an idea springs to mind, an idea that could make your passage through the Darklands much easier and greatly increase the chances for your mission's success.

Turn to **271**.

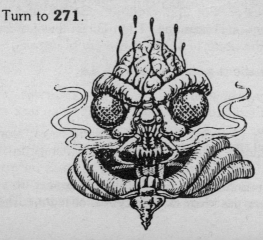

336

Your arrow strikes the Drakkar horseman but wounds him only superficially, merely grazing the side of his neck. However, the sudden pain makes him cry out and snatch the reins to his chest. His startled horse rears up on its hind legs, throwing its rider to the ground. You drop your bow and draw a hand weapon before leaping upon the prone Drakkar, determined to finish him before he has a chance to recover.

Turn to **175**.

337 – *Illustration XIX*

Your first blow shatters the skull of one bird, sending it cartwheeling wildly across the surface of the sea before finally death stills it. The remaining bird shrieks in alarm, but rather than take fright and fly away, it hovers above you as if waiting for the right moment to strike. With a chilling caw, it darts towards you, determined to exact its revenge for the death of its mate.

Sea-scavenger: COMBAT SKILL 22   ENDURANCE 10

This creature is immune to Mindblast (but not Psi-surge).

If you win the combat, turn to **14**.

338

The creature smiles, bows, then shuffles away along the corridor, a quiet sniggering sound issuing from his thin mouth as he makes his way towards an iron-runged staircase. You watch him disappear up the stairs, then you close and lock your cabin door. Tired

XIX.   The sea-scavenger darts towards you

and hungry, you must now eat a Meal or lose 3 ENDURANCE points before you can settle down to sleep.

After several hours, you awake to the sound of a loud click, barely audible above the increased din of the Lajakeka's engine, and at once you sense that your cabin door has just closed. Swiftly you rise from the bunk and rush to the door, hoping to catch a glimpse of whoever, or whatever, gained access to your room while you were asleep.

If you possess the Magnakai Discipline of Animal Control, and have reached the Kai rank of Mentora or higher, turn to **273**.

If you do not possess this skill, or have yet to reach this level of Kai training, turn to **98**.

Your quarters turn out to be cramped and smelly, sandwiched between the ship's galley and the bilge. Despite the lack of space, and a stomach-churning smell redolent of dead fish, you manage to snatch a few hours' sleep before you are awoken by a grey dawn haze filtering through the grimy glass of the cabin's solitary porthole.

Up on deck the captain stands alone at the forecastle rail, scanning the empty horizon through his telescope. You join him and take the opportunity to deliver the envelope you are carrying.

' 'Tis a brave and risky venture you've committed yourself to, comrade,' he says, his grey eyes devouring the words of the parchment, bearing the seal of the Brotherhood of the Crystal Star, which he finds folded inside. 'Yet these be risky times. I can only surmise what lies beyond your journey to Dejkaata, but of one thing you can be sure — I will do all in my power to see you safely there.'

Immediately he issues orders to turn the ship about and steer a new course — north-by-north west. The crew react to the sudden change of plan with great speculation, yet, despite the dangers they know they may face, none challenge their captain's decision or voice dissent.

Turn to **241**.

340

You spring forward and strike a blow that would have decapitated a mortal creature. But the moment your weapon hits Taktaal's flesh, it disintegrates in a flash of sparks. The Darklord laughs as he closes his clawed hands around your throat and squeezes the life from your body.

Tragically, your life and your mission end here in the Tower of the Damned.

341

You try to dodge the spinning blade, but you trip over the body of the dead Drakkarim gunner and the sword hits you squarely in the chest. White-hot pain engulfs you like a raging fire, burning your body and numbing your limbs. It reaches its zenith, then disappears as, reluctantly, you surrender to death.

Your life and your mission end here.

342 – *Illustration XX*

You turn to run but your exit is blocked by a squat, horny-skinned creature with baleful, milky-coloured eyes. These eyes roll like balls of mist inside its head as it advances on you slowly, an axe of black steel held in its clawed hands, poised to strike you down.

Xaghash: COMBAT SKILL 32   ENDURANCE 42

If you possess the sword, Helshezag, and wish to use it, remember to add the appropriate bonuses to your COMBAT SKILL.

If you possess the Sommerswerd, and wish to use it, turn to **208**.

If you win the combat, turn to **106**.

343

Your killing blow sends the Ictakko spiralling towards the ceiling, twisting and weaving like a punctured balloon. It crashes into a cluster of stalactites, impaling itself on the spear-like formations and dislodging them with the impact of its vast weight. For a fleeting second, you glimpse the creatures's ghastly features – its pear-shaped horny head and bulb-tipped antennae; its spider-like abdomen and transparent wings – before it plummets into the cold, inky darkness of the crevasse.

Turn to **87**.

344

The creature strikes and you dive aside, inches from a gruesome death in its powerful jaws. Snapping repeatedly it twists its supple neck to follow your escape across the shattered, body-strewn planks, and lunges

XX. The Xaghash advances towards you, its axe poised to
strike you down

again when you reach the stairs that lead to the stern deck. This time you save your skin by pulling yourself into the rigging, and, as you are climbing aloft, you see the Xargath crash through the stairs and into the hull. It tries to withdraw its head but it cannot: it is held firm, trapped among the splintered timbers. This may be your only opportunity to defeat this terror before it breaks free and drags the ship to the bottom of the sea.

If you wish to attack the Xargath while its head is trapped in the wreckage, turn to **35**.

If you wish to avoid combat by hiding in the crow's nest, turn to **277**.

345

The tube proves difficult to remove from its mounting, but you manage to prise it loose with a strip of steel which you find lying at your feet. You invert it and reconnect its copper cables, but the moment that the last cable is brought into contact, there is a blinding flash of white light and you are engulfed by a blast of flame and twisted metal. Your act of sabotage has set off an explosion which has completely destroyed the ironclad juggernaut and half of Argazad harbour, but it has cost you your life and sealed the doom of Magnamund.

Your life and your quest end here.

346

A curved steel door slides shut, sealing the entrance, and plunging the gloomy chamber into total darkness. Then a narrow column of yellowy light pours on to your head, and a man's voice, loud and full of arrogance, shatters the silence.

'What brings you here, Drakkar?' he booms, filling the chamber with resounding echoes. He speaks a curious dialect of Giak that sounds vaguely familiar. It is a dialect common in Magador, a border territory now occupied by Darkland armies. 'I seek the Slavemaster,' you answer. 'I have come from Argazad to report that Sommerlund is burning!'

'That is welcome news indeed,' comes the reply, in a tone far less severe.

The steel door slides open and your Giak escort are dismissed. As it clangs shut behind them, the light grows brighter until you can see clearly the man to whom you have just spoken.

Turn to **81**.

347

You shoulder your bow and draw a hand weapon just in time to meet your enemies' attack. They swarm around you, howling with primal fury, their teeth bared and their faces contorted by hatred, as they raise their swords to cut you down.

Drakkarim Marines:
COMBAT SKILL 29   ENDURANCE 40

If you win the combat, turn to **28**.

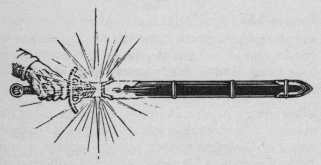

348

The Liganim draws level with your hiding place then halts. Suddenly a tingling sensation ripples your scalp, as a wave of psychic energy washes over your mind. The Liganim turns his head and holds you with his cruel gaze, probing your thoughts. He finds what he is looking for: you are an imposter. He gives a high-pitched shriek and snatches a dagger from his belt as he hurls himself maniacally upon you.

Liganim: COMBAT SKILL 25   ENDURANCE 26

Unless you possess the Magnakai Discipline of Psi-screen, deduct 1 ENDURANCE point at the beginning of every round of combat, owing to the creature's persistent psychic attacks.

If you win the combat, turn to **246**.

349

Your speedy dispatch of the guards buys you precious time in which to escape from the outpost and disappear among the rocks and crags that line the roadway through the pass. Loudly the alarm bell echoes between the walls of solid rock, its dreadful clang reverberating in your head. You run for more than an hour before the sound fades completely.

Turn to **137**.

350

Only a circle of fire-scorched steel marks the spot where Darklord Gnaag finally met his doom. You look upon this patch of twisted metal and your spirits soar with the realization that you have defeated your archenemy in mortal combat. But your mission is yet to be completed. Quickly you remove the Crystal Explosive from your backpack and approach the Transfusor. You place it in position, next to a shaft connected to the Lake of Blood from which the device draws its power. Once the crystal is primed, you hurry out of the chamber through the archway by which Gnaag entered. Guided by your instincts, you find your way around the tower to the oval landing platform, and to the means of escape from the Black City which awaits you there – Gnaag's Imperial Zlanbeast.

You are high above the city, steering the reluctant Zlanbeast eastwards to Aarnak, when the crystal detonates. Within moments it starts a chain reaction, which destroys the Transfusor, reduces Helgedad to a fiery holocaust of shattered granite and twisted steel, and brings about the rapid demise of the Darklords and their armies scattered throughout Magnamund.

Your victory is total. At last you have fulfilled your destiny to avenge the Kai and rid your land of the evil that has threatened her for thousands of years. You return to Sommerlund a conquering hero, and, as Kai Grand Master, you begin the task of restoring the Kai to their former glory. The chronicle of your struggle against the Darklords will pass into legend, inspiring future generations of Kai warriors to keep alive your ideals of bravery, skill and selfless courage. Yet the saga that is the story of your life does not end here. In future times the chronicle will tell of the adventures you undertook during your Kai Grand Mastership. Until the time comes for their telling, may the Gods Ishir and Kai watch over you, Grand Master Lone Wolf, hero and saviour of Sommerlund.

A ROLE-PLAYING ADVENTURE!

LONE WOLF

YOU are Lone Wolf!

by Joe Dever and Gary Chalk

__Flight From the Dark	0-425-08436-1/$3.99
__Fire on the Water	0-425-08437-X/$3.99
__The Caverns of Kalte	0-425-09357-3/$3.99
__The Chasm of Doom	0-425-08419-1/$3.99
__Shadow on the Sand	0-425-08440-X/$3.50
__The Kingdom of Terror	0-425-08446-9/$3.99
__Castle Death	0-425-10014-6/$3.99
__Jungle of Horrors	0-425-10484-2/$3.99
__The Cauldron of Fear	0-425-10848-1/$3.99
__The Dungeons of Torgar	0-425-10930-5/$3.50
__The Prisoners of Time	0-425-11568-2/$3.50
__The Masters of Darkness	0-425-11718-0/$3.99
__The Plague Lords of Ruel	0-425-13245-5/$3.99
__The Captives of Kaag	0-425-13304-4/$3.50

For Visa, MasterCard and American Express
orders ($15 minimum) call: 1-800-631-8571

Check book(s). Fill out coupon. Send to:
BERKLEY PUBLISHING GROUP
390 Murray Hill Pkwy., Dept. B
East Rutherford, NJ 07073

NAME———————————————————

ADDRESS————————————————

CITY ———————————————————

STATE——————— ZIP————————

PLEASE ALLOW 6 WEEKS FOR DELIVERY.
PRICES ARE SUBJECT TO CHANGE WITHOUT NOTICE.

POSTAGE AND HANDLING:
$1.75 for one book, 75¢ for each
additional. Do not exceed $5.50.

BOOK TOTAL $ _____

POSTAGE & HANDLING $ _____

APPLICABLE SALES TAX $ _____
(CA, NJ, NY, PA)

TOTAL AMOUNT DUE $ _____

PAYABLE IN US FUNDS.
(No cash orders accepted.)

235a

The World of
LONE WOLF

One of the most exciting fantasy role-playing adventures ever!
by Joe Dever and Ian Page

You are Grey Star the Wizard, masterful hero of the Lone Wolf series. As you set out to free the land of your birth from the Wytch-King's savage rule, or travel to distant, hostile countries, you must make the decisions and fight the combats, using the unique powers and courage of the Wizard

___GREY STAR THE WIZARD	0-425-09590-8/$3.99
___THE FORBIDDEN CITY	0-425-09710-2/$3.50
___BEYOND THE NIGHTMARE GATE	0-425-09892-3/$3.50
___WAR OF THE WIZARDS	0-425-10539-3/$3.99

For Visa, Master Card and American Express orders ($15 minimum) call: 1-800-631-8571 Check book(s). Fill out coupon. Send to:

BERKLEY PUBLISHING GROUP
390 Murray Hill Pkwy., Dept. B
East Rutherford, NJ 07073

NAME _____

ADDRESS _____

CITY _____

STATE _____ZIP _____

PLEASE ALLOW 6 WEEKS FOR DELIVERY.
PRICES ARE SUBJECT TO CHANGE WITHOUT NOTICE.

POSTAGE AND HANDLING:
$1.75 for one book, 75¢ for each additional. Do not exceed $5.50.

BOOK TOTAL	$ _____
POSTAGE & HANDLING	$ _____
APPLICABLE SALES TAX (CA, NJ, NY, PA)	$ _____
TOTAL AMOUNT DUE	$ _____

PAYABLE IN US FUNDS.
(No cash orders accepted.)

238

RANDOM NUMBER TABLE

8	2	4	1	3	1	7	9	6	2
6	8	6	5	4	3	8	7	8	1
9	5	6	6	5	7	6	3	1	7
5	2	4	0	6	8	8	6	3	2
0	5	9	5	7	9	0	4	1	4
2	8	5	2	3	6	7	2	6	5
4	8	0	4	8	7	1	3	4	0
6	2	0	4	4	1	6	1	2	0
8	4	1	2	6	5	6	1	0	6
4	6	5	0	9	0	5	9	5	7

COMBAT RULES SUMMARY

1. Add your COMBAT SKILL to any extra points given to you by your Kai Disciplines.

2. Subtract the COMBAT SKILL of your enemy from this total. This number = Combat Ratio.

3. Pick number from *Random Number Table*.

4. Turn to *Combat Results Tables*.

5. Find your Combat Ratio on the top of chart and cross reference to random number you have picked. (*E* indicates loss of ENDURANCE points to Enemy. LW indicates loss of ENDURANCE points to Lone Wolf.)

6. Continue the combat from Stage 3 until one character is dead. This is when ENDURANCE points of either character fall to 0.

TO EVADE COMBAT

1. You may only do this when the text of the adventure offers you the opportunity.

2. You undertake one round of combat in the usual way. All points lost by the enemy are ignored, only Lone Wolf loses the ENDURANCE points.

3. If the book offers the chance of taking evasive action in place of combat, it can be taken in the first round of combat or any subsequent round.

COMBAT RES

Combat Ratio

Random Number	−11 OR GREATER	−10/−9	−8/−7	−6/−5	−4/−3	−2/−1
1	E −0	E −0	E −0	E −0	E −1	E −2
	LW K	LW K	LW −8	LW −6	LW −6	LW −5
2	E −0	E −0	E −0	E −1	E −2	E −3
	LW K	LW −8	LW −7	LW −6	LW −5	LW −5
3	E −0	E −0	E −1	E −2	E −3	E −4
	LW −8	LW −7	LW −6	LW −5	LW −5	LW −4
4	E −0	E −1	E −2	E −3	E −4	E −5
	LW −8	LW −7	LW −6	LW −5	LW −4	LW −4
5	E −1	E −2	E −3	E −4	E −5	E −6
	LW −7	LW −6	LW −5	LW −4	LW −4	LW −3
6	E −2	E −3	E −4	E −5	E −6	E −7
	LW −6	LW −6	LW −5	LW −4	LW −3	LW −2
7	E −3	E −4	E −5	E −6	E −7	E −8
	LW −5	LW −5	LW −4	LW −3	LW −2	LW −2
8	E −4	E −5	E −6	E −7	E −8	E −9
	LW −4	LW −4	LW −3	LW −2	LW −1	LW −1
9	E −5	E −6	E −7	E −8	E −9	E −10
	LW −3	LW −3	LW −2	LW −0	LW −0	LW −0
0	E −6	E −7	E −8	E −9	E −10	E −11
	LW −0	LW −0	LW −0	LW −0	LW −0	LW −0

E = ENEMY LW = LONE WOLF